Donald MacKenzie and The Murder Room

›› This title is part of The Murder Room, our series dedicated to making available out-of-print or hard-to-find titles by classic crime writers.

Crime fiction has always held up a mirror to society. The Victorians were fascinated by sensational murder and the emerging science of detection; now we are obsessed with the forensic detail of violent death. And no other genre has so captivated and enthralled readers.

Vast troves of classic crime writing have for a long time been unavailable to all but the most dedicated frequenters of second-hand bookshops. The advent of digital publishing means that we are now able to bring you the backlists of a huge range of titles by classic and contemporary crime writers, some of which have been out of print for decades.

From the genteel amateur private eyes of the Golden Age and the femmes fatales of pulp fiction, to the morally ambiguous hard-boiled detectives of mid twentieth-century America and their descendants who walk our twenty-first century streets, The Murder Room has it all. ››

The Murder Room
Where Criminal Minds Meet

themurderroom.com

Donald MacKenzie 1908–1994

Donald MacKenzie was born in Ontario, Canada, and educated in England, Canada and Switzerland. For twenty-five years MacKenzie lived by crime in many countries. 'I went to jail,' he wrote, 'if not with depressing regularity, too often for my liking.' His last sentences were five years in the United States and three years in England, running consecutively. He began writing and selling stories when in American jail. 'I try to do exactly as I like as often as possible and I don't think I'm either psychopathic, a wayward boy, a problem of our time, a charming rogue. Or ever was.'

He had a wife, Estrela, and a daughter, and they divided their time between England, Portugal, Spain and Austria.

By Donald MacKenzie

Raven's Revenge

Donald MacKenzie

An Orion book

Copyright © The Estate of Donald MacKenzie 1982

The right of Donald MacKenzie to be identified as the author of this work has been asserted in accordance with the Copyright, Designs and Patents Act 1988.

This edition published by
The Orion Publishing Group Ltd
Orion House
5 Upper St Martin's Lane
London WC2H 9EA

An Hachette UK company
A CIP catalogue record for this book is available from the British Library

ISBN 978 1 4719 0511 7

www.orionbooks.co.uk

For Sarah, for your sense of humour and music.

For Sarah, for your sense of humour and music.

Two passengers who hated one another were in the same boat. One was sitting in the bow, the other in the stern. A storm came over and when the ship was on the point of sinking, the man in the stern asked the steersman which part of the boat would go under water first. On being told that the bow would go first, he replied, "I do not mind dying myself if I can see my enemy die before me."

Many men do not care what happens to themselves as long as they see their enemies suffer first. (Aesop's Fables)

Prologue

IT WAS JUNE and the sunshine had lingered, warming wherever it touched. Kirstie was in her bikini, collecting the crab shells. They had eaten at four, lying side by side out on deck. There was fruit in a basket, beer in the portable cooler. Raven's only exercise had been to answer the doorbell, letting in Jerry Soo.

Raven looked at his watch as the street lights came on. Well-cut diamonds traced the outlines of the bridges.

"Twenty past nine! Do you realize that we haven't done a goddam thing all day?"

"Speak for yourselves," said Soo. He was still in his striped flannel suit and tie, dropping pieces of bread in the water that the fish ignored. "I've been hard at it since eight o'clock this morning."

Kirstie disappeared with the remnants of their meal. Raven rolled over on the sun-bed as Soo continued.

"I heard that Drake's wife just divorced him."

He opened a can of beer, drank, and wiped his mouth on the back of his hand. Raven took the half-empty can and finished it.

"I wonder it wasn't the other way around," he said. "Wasn't she supposed to be having a fling with someone on the Drugs Squad?"

Kirstie stepped back on deck. She had tied a kanga around the lower part of her body and pulled her taffy-colored hair into a bun. Her face was disapproving as she looked from Raven to Soo.

1

"You men make me sick! You're worse than women for gossip."

Raven winked at his friend. "We take things like that very seriously, marriage and divorce."

Soo leaned against the superstructure. "He's been transferred to Winchester Prison. He's working outside the walls. He could walk at any time."

Raven reached for a cigarette and pulled Kirstie down beside him. "Let him walk." He put his arm around Kirstie's warm shoulders and touched her bare skin with his lips. "You smell of suntan oil and crab. It's an interesting mixture."

She smiled more these days. "Remind me to take your picture tomorrow. In this light you're almost presentable."

"Jesus!" Soo straightened up on his short bandy legs. "I don't think I can take any more of this. We'll see you people next week. Don't bother getting up. I'll let myself out."

The gangway door slammed. A couple of minutes later they heard the rattle of the departing Volkswagen. They lay still and close, their eyes exploring one another, lulled by the gentle movement of the boat. The violet light gave her face softness.

"Know something," he said impulsively. "I don't ever want to forget today."

She grinned. "You mean you're happy, sharing your life with a woman who refuses to do as she's told? It won't be the same, you know, not always."

"It never is," he said and released her hand. "Come on, let's go to bed."

1

THE RINGING of the telephone pried Raven loose from his sleep. He reached for the receiver, looking up blearily at the clock on the bedside table. It was twenty-five minutes past eight and the sky was still dark outside. A gull screamed like a banshee nearby.

The chop-suey accent was chipper. "Mistah Laven?"

Raven rolled over on his back and closed his eyes. "For God's sake, Jerry, this is Sunday morning!" Jerry Soo would be speaking from his penthouse apartment on the other side of the river. The building could just about be seen on a clear day, a splash of ocher against the dove-gray of the warehouses.

The Hong Kong cop took the reproach lightly. "What's the matter, you people have too much to drink last night?"

Raven tried to clear his head. He could see Kirstie in the kitchen, dwarfed in his blue-toweling robe, and he could smell eggs and bacon frying. She came to the kitchen door, holding up the percolator for him to see. When Kirstie was in residence they drank coffee at breakfast. Alone, he drank tea.

"It's Jerry," he told her.

"Well, don't hang up until I've had a word with Louise. I haven't spoken with her in weeks," she said.

Her shoulder-length hair was the color of pale tobacco and tied in a loose knot behind her ears. She had a knack of appearing as fresh as a blade of spring grass no matter what hell she might have been raising the night before. He couldn't remember anyone ever claiming that Kirstie was beautiful although with her wide-set eyes and long-legged body she had a coltish charm. The trouble was that they seemed to be sniping at one another recently. But, looking at her, Raven decided that she was still as close to his ideal as any woman he had known.

He relayed her message and gave her Soo's answer. "Louise is in Edinburgh. She won't be back until the twelfth of next month." Louise Soo was a cellist with the Philharmonic Orchestra.

Raven snuggled back under the bedclothes. The houseboat had been double-glazed during the summer, sliding doors and electrically operated curtains fitted throughout the superstructure. Candles now burned without guttering and even Mrs. Burrows, a determined opponent of change, allowed the improvement. There was less dust, she said grudgingly.

Soo chatted along. "Guess who showed up on the Discharged Prisoners List?"

The mimeographed sheet was circulated to all Scotland Yard squads and gave the names of convicted men due for release from jail. Raven stretched his legs, wincing. His varicose veins had been giving him trouble and he'd had them injected the day before.

"Anyone I know?" he asked.

"George Drake," said Soo.

"Indeed," said Raven.

"Indeed," repeated Soo. "And remembering what he threatened to do to you I thought you'd like to know."

The memory went back twelve years when Raven had still been on the force, a Detective-Inspector working out of Scotland Yard. His meeting with Commander Drake had been in the line of duty, a junior officer consulting his superior. For reasons that Raven had never fully established Drake had taken a strong dislike to him. Over the next few years he did his best to ruin Raven's career. Circumstances led to Raven's resignation. There was irony in the fact that shortly afterward

Raven was the means of putting Drake behind bars.

"How long did he do in the end?" asked Raven.

"Five years and six months."

Memory recaptured another scene, Number One courtroom at the Old Bailey. Drake had just heard his sentence and, ashen-faced under the strobes, was staring across at Raven. The two warders tried to move Drake but he clung to the rail of the dock. His voice was suddenly loud in the hushed courtroom.

"I'll be back, Raven!" he said. "I'll be back to take care of you!"

Raven scratched the back of his neck. "Ah well. The air's going to smell a lot less pleasant."

"According to the sheet he was released on Friday," said Soo.

"He's probably in a wheelchair," said Raven. "He must be seventy."

"Sixty-two," said Soo. "Just keep your eyes open. He's a vindictive bastard."

Raven yawned. Smell of the food was giving him an appetite. "Was that all you wanted to say?"

"You're not only ungrateful," said Soo. "You're discourteous. When are we going to play some more squash?"

"Probably never," said Raven. "You're talking to someone who is slowly being stripped of his manhood. I had to go to Doctor West yesterday. Injections for my varicose veins."

"Acupuncture," Soo said briskly. "I'll introduce you to a Chinese practitioner. Acupuncture cures all ills, including afflictions of the wind and water. Kiss that lovely lady of yours for me."

Raven swung his legs from the bed, shaking his head as he inspected his calves. The swellings in the knotted veins were reduced but he knew in his heart that the next step would be surgery. They would rearrange his circulation and put him in bed surrounded by withering fruit and books that he had read before.

He donned his pajamas, brushed his teeth, and limped into

the kitchen. Kirstie had had the room repapered a shade of yellow that brightened the cheerlessness of winter. A vase filled with her favorite freesias scented the whole boat. She had collected the Sunday newspapers from the box at the end of the gangway. She put a plate of food in front of him and sat down nibbbling a piece of toast.

"What was all that about?" she demanded.

He removed the white from the two fried eggs and dropped it in the wastebasket.

"What coffee is this?"

"It's the same that we've been drinking for months. I brought it from Paris." She looked at him over her cup. "What did Jerry want?"

It was quiet up on the embankment. London was still sunk in its weekend torpor. He shrugged.

"Nothing much. He just wanted to tell me that a man has been released from prison."

She lifted her cup, the sleeves of the robe sliding down her arms. "What man?"

"A guy I helped put inside. Someone called Drake." He speared a piece of bacon and dunked it in the yoke.

"You just dropped egg on your pajama top," she said. She had already eaten her breakfast. Five feet nine inches tall, she had weighed 130 pounds for twelve years. She ate and drank what she liked and was the envy of women who had to watch their figures. The frown lines at the corners of her eyes were white against the faded tan. "I remember," she said. "That's the man who threatened you in the courtroom. Commander Drake. What did Jerry say about him?"

The *Albatross* rolled in the swell of a passing boat. Raven wiped his mouth.

"Not a lot. You know how Jerry fusses."

"No," she said coolly. "I do not know how Jerry fusses. In fact I'd say Jerry's about as fussy as a bum at a barbecue."

"O.K., O.K.," he said, lifting a hand in defeat. "Why don't we talk about something else?"

She put her elbows on the table and leaned her chin on her hands. "What would you like to talk about?"

It was the wrong thing to have said and he saw the trap too late.

"Marriage and having babies?" she asked.

He reached for the newspapers. "Look, darling. I'm still hung over and my legs hurt. Added to which we've covered that ground 943 times."

She was ringing him out with her eyes. "Anything that matters to me you don't want to discuss. You never have."

He threw the papers back on the table. "That just isn't true. You weren't talking about marriage and babies three years ago."

"True," she replied. "I still hoped that it would be you who would raise the topic."

He shook his head slowly. "If you're trying to make me feel like a shit you're succeeding. But I can't help the way I am. I never wanted the sort of responsibilities you're talking about and you knew it. Please don't let's fight!"

She took a deep breath. "I'm not too sure how to say this, John. I don't know what's happening but it isn't good. I worry about us but especially I worry about you."

It was light now outside and the gulls were noisy on the mudflats. "I haven't changed," he said. "I'm still the same."

She reached across and took his hand. "That's part of the problem. I'm *asking* you to change. You always said that you wanted to buy a boat and sail. 'The wild west wind,' remember? Well, *do* it! We can go together. No more talk about babies or marriage. Just you and I doing something together before it's too late."

Her hand was warm on his and he smiled. "I know what brought this on. You think I'm going to be in trouble with Drake, don't you? Well, forget it. He's just another con as far as I'm concerned. I must have put a couple of hundred inside in my time. If I lost sleep when each one threatened me I'd be in worse shape than I am."

She freed her hand and carried the breakfast things to the sink. "Well," he said. "I'm going back to bed. Do you want to come?"

She swung around, her face neither happy nor sad. "*La douche anglaise*," she said. "Just keep it up and you won't have any friends left. Not even me."

He shrugged, walked into the bedroom, and drew the curtains.

2

DRAKE WAS SITTING on the bench outside the Governor's office under the eye of his escort, a large man with an aggressive mustache and several fancy ways of standing. The one currently employed was with the legs splayed, shoulders squared, and hands clasped behind the back. The eyes were allowed to rove but snapped back on the slightest pretext. The end result denoted vigilance. The toes of the guard's boots were brilliantly polished and reflected the light from the overhead lamp.

The escort sprang to attention as a voice called from behind the door. He grabbed the handle, flashed a salute, and motioned Drake to his feet. "Give your full name and number to the Prison Governor!"

It was half-past four on a gray November afternoon. The man behind the desk looked up at the guard. "Thank you, Mr. Hancock. You may close the door behind you."

Drake stayed on his feet in front of the desk. "One seven six eight, George Drake." He omitted the customary "sir."

The Governor indicated a chair. He was a shrimp-faced man in his fifties wearing a crumpled tweed suit. It was the first time that Drake had been in the office since he arrived. Large windows overlooked the formal gardens in front of the administration building. A coal fire was burning in the grate. The room was decorated with artifacts made by the prisoners. Matchstick sculptures, paintings done in the style of Grandma Moses, model schooners ingeniously erected in glass bottles. The carpet was worn, the furniture without distinction. In spite of this there was an impression of comfort and warmth after the cheerlessness of the cells and corridors.

Drake settled back in his chair, a pugnacious-looking man with a high complexion and hair the color of fresh steel-filings. He was wearing the prison uniform of rough gray flannel and clumsy shoes.

The Governor smiled. "The big day, eh?"

Drake hid his dislike, determined that he would jump through no hoops. Barring a flagrant disregard of prison rules there was nothing more that they could do to him. He had made no application for parole, aware of the Board's sensitivity to public opinion. A crooked cop stood about as much chance of making parole as a child-molester.

Drake stared out through the window as the Govenor opened Drake's prison record. It was all there, thought Drake. The memorial of a man's suffering, as detailed and complete as the bastards could make it. Medical history, work record, the snide remarks by chaplain and staff, all the useless comments designed to boost the sense of authority.

The Governor pulled his chair away from the fire. "You puzzle me, Drake. You've done good time, all the right things. In fact you haven't made a wrong move since you came here. But you've volunteered for nothing. No evening classes, no organized recreations."

Drake showed stained dentures. "That's what you told me when I arrived. 'Keep your nose clean and stay out of trouble.'"

The Governor flashed a man-to-man smile. "You've done that all right! But then I suppose you're the sort of chap who would have done it in any case. A man doesn't reach the position you held in the police force without knowing the way to go about things."

"Low cunning," said Drake.

The Governor looked slightly uncomfortable. "Do you have any complaints to make about your treatment here?"

Drake grinned. "You've got to be joking. The time to complain is when something happens. No, I don't have any complaints to make."

"This isn't the sort of establishment I'd like to be running." The Governor's manner was almost confidential. "But rules are rules."

Drake's burly shoulders lifted. "It's hardly my choice either."

"I suppose not. We're not really communicating, are we?"

"You're talking, I'm listening," Drake said indifferently.

The Governor thought about this for a moment. "Yes," he agreed. "I suppose that's about the size of it. You know, I joined the prison service with all the right intentions. I had big ideas of being a reformer. I hadn't reckoned with the system. It's hard to run even a minimum security jail like this and remain a human being."

Drake was having a field day. "It's difficult to wear a number on your sleeve and remain a human being."

The Governor's smile was tired. "I know that, too. What I want you to understand is that when a man leaves this place I'm genuinely concerned about what happens to him."

"That shouldn't give you too much trouble," said Drake. "Most of them are only out on temporary leave of absence."

He was sixty-two years old but all things considered he had never felt better in his life. For the last eighteen months he had been working in the open air. A sense of well-being made him indulgent.

The Governor was leafing through Drake's record again. Lights came on in the yards outside, throwing sharp shadows across the concrete walks. The first yelps sounded from the dog kennels.

"You don't seem to have written many letters since you came here." The Governor's tone was curious.

"Three," said Drake. All had been to his lawyer.

A coal settled in the grate, sending up a spurt of colored gas. The Governor had reached Drake's medical history.

"There's a recommendation here that you see a heart specialist."

Drake measured his answer. "That's a recommendation that could have been made four years ago. My heart's in no worse condition now than it was then. I'll survive."

The Governor closed the record. "Why didn't you want to see the After Care representative?"

"That's simple," said Drake. "He didn't have anything to offer that I wanted."

The Governor's smile was wry. "I've got a strong feeling that I'm being put in my place. In fact it's times like this when I know that I can't be doing my job properly."

Drake gave him no help at all. The prick wanted some sort of breast-beating, something to get him off the hook.

The Governor rose and stuck out his hand. "The best of luck to you in any case."

"Thanks," said Drake, ignoring the outstretched hand.

Prisoners due for release spent their last night in the Reception Wing, isolated from the general population. Drake stood naked in the office, aware of a sagging belly and flesh that was beginning to crepe. The jailer searched him thoroughly and threw him a sheet. The idea was that Drake would take nothing out of the jail that he had not brought in with him.

The jailer was running late and anxious to get home. "First cell on your right," he said. "Chuck out the sheet and rack yourself up!"

Drake closed the cell door. A couple of minutes later he heard the gate clang. He would be alone now until they brought his supper. Lights were burning in the main wings. The cons would be returning from labor at any time.

His civilian clothing was on the bed, the blue serge suit and scuffed black boots. An envelope on the table contained his personal property. It was strange looking at things he hadn't seen in years, the articles he had had in his pockets when he was arrested. The police had kept his address book, the clowns. If they thought that it might still be of use to them, forget it. He had been at the game for too long and could still run rings around the best of them. It was a fact that they'd be learning soon enough.

He went through the rest of his belongings. The house in Forest Hill had gone to his wife as part of the divorce settlement. Knowing Mildred the first thing she would have done would be to have the locks changed. He still smiled, imagining her face when she learned that the house was mortgaged. The flight ticket to Brazil was six years out of date.

He shifted his clothes off the bed and stretched out on it, the Yale key between his fingers. Including the time spent awaiting trial he had spent sixty-six months in jail. Everything he had planned for had been destroyed by one man in the space of a few short days. His instincts had been right about Raven in the first place. The man wasn't just a college-boy cop, an idiot with an upper-class accent. He was a maniac who fancied himself as some sort of avenging angel.

Drake locked his arms behind his head and closed his eyes. From the moment of his arrest he had never let Raven get far from his thoughts. He could still smell the acrid smoke, hear the fake fire alarm that had flushed him out of his hiding place no more than hours away from freedom. His lips thinned. Name whatever was bad that had happened to him, Raven was responsible for it.

No matter what people said, revenge was a rewarding emotion. He was sixty-two years old with neither family nor friends to care about, nothing to stop him devoting the rest of his life to Raven's destruction. He had a brain, purpose, and money and had suffered too many humiliations to fail now.

He slept fitfully, waking at twenty to six. He dressed and

sat in the chilly cell waiting for the first jangle of keys. A jailer on night shift brought Drake's breakfast. He left the congealing bacon, contenting himself with the mug of stewed tea. The jail clock was striking eight as he was escorted across the cobbled courtyard. A jailer unlocked the outer door and Drake stepped out to freedom.

The buildings and streets were touched with cold damp, the gutters choked with fallen leaves. Everything was strange, including the air, laden as it was with the taint of dead bonfires. He walked on down the hill, his starved senses registering new impressions. Children on their way to school, the gleam of horses' hindquarters. He passed a couple of guards walking to work, his look canceling their tentative greetings.

He was downtown now, in the center of the small cathedral city. He bought a newspaper and walked across the railroad station lobby. The London train was due in twelve minutes. He had been given a travel voucher that he dropped in a wastebasket. He bought himself a first class ticket for Victoria, crossed the bridge, and joined the passengers waiting on the track. The women fascinated him after years of segregation. Mildred had informed his lawyer that she had donated his clothes to the Red Cross. He was carrying a brown-paper package containing a change of underwear. That and what he had on constituted his entire wardrobe.

The crossties shook and he moved forward, finding an empty compartment and closing the door firmly. The carriage stank of stale tobacco smoke and the floor was littered with butts. He threw his homburg up on the rack and lowered the window a couple of inches. British Rail had not changed.

He remained undisturbed all the way to Victoria except for the visit of a ticket collector. At ten minutes to ten, he was shouldering his way through the crowd waiting to board. His feeling of strangeness dwindled with every step that he took. Landmarks evoked memories. Scotland Yard was hidden by the soaring mass of Westminster Hall. He walked along Wilton Road, turned into a doorway and climbed a flight of stairs. A brass plate on a door read:

WATES AND WARBECK
SOLICITORS AND COMMISSIONERS FOR OATHS

Drake opened the door. A blonde with a drowned, blank look raised her face from the typewriter. The fact that Drake still had his hat on clearly offended her.

"Mr. Warbeck," he said.

She spoke through a handkerchief pressed against her lips. "Do you have an appointment?"

"No," said Drake. "All you have to do is tell him that George Drake is here."

She removed the handkerchief and her voice was tart. "Mr. Warbeck is with a client."

Drake kept his patience. "I'm a client too. Now be a good girl and do as you're told."

She picked up the phone. When she put it down again, discretion had gotten the better of her resentment.

"Mr. Warbeck will be right out."

The door opened on a man as neat in attire as Drake was slovenly. The lawyer was in his late forties. He came forward, his hand out in welcome, an effusive smile on his face.

"George! How nice to see you!" He glanced at his watch and frowned. "Just give me a few minutes to get rid of this other person."

"Don't bother," said Drake. "All I need is the key."

Warbeck lowered his voice. "But I kept myself free for lunch. I thought we'd have a bite together, relax. Talk things over."

"There's nothing to talk about," said Drake.

Warbeck spread his hands. "Whatever you say. I'll get the key."

Drake turned his back on the blonde. Warbeck had defended

14

him at his trial and Drake had retained him to handle his divorce. The lawyer returned with a sealed envelope.

Drake took it. "I'll be in touch," he promised.

"Do you have an address?" asked Warbeck.

"I'll be in touch," Drake repeated and lifted a hand in farewell.

He opened the envelope on the way downstairs. Inside was a finely tooled key with the letters E.S.D. stamped on the shank and a number. He hailed a cab and leaned back hard against the upholstery.

"Drop me off on the corner of Exbury Street."

Retaining the key had changed the course of his life. It had been hidden in the heel of his boot for two months prior to his arrest. They had stripped him at the police station, his colleagues making the body search as humiliating as possible. Once in his cell in Brixton Prison, Drake had retrieved the key and passed it to Warbeck in court. It was an incident that the lawyer had never since referred to.

The cab stopped and Drake paid off the driver. He strolled a couple of blocks, looking in shop windows, making sudden abrupt turns. He detected nothing suspicious, no suggestion that he was being tagged. He crossed the street, climbed the steps to the bank, and gave his password to an official at the desk. The man recorded the date and time of Drake's visit and accompanied him down to the vaults. A guard pressed a button that allowed the two men to pass beyond a heavy steel grille. The doors to the strong room were eight feet by four and nine inches thick. Inside each strong room were four hundred boxes. The bank official used his key first. Drake followed. Neither key opened the box without the other.

Now Drake was alone. Inside the steel drawer were a New Zealand passport and driving license. Both documents were currently valid. In addition to these, there were nineteen thousand dollars in cash and a checkbook on a bank in Basel. Last of all was a tape cassette. He put the cassette in his pocket.

The police had located his British bank account and the judge had made a confiscation order for its contents. But they had missed the Swiss account. He still had the best part of a hundred thousand pounds, more than enough to finance his plans for the future.

He took five thousand dollars, the passport, and driving license and locked the drawer again. Then he signed the book and made his way down the steps to the street. It was ten-thirty. There was plenty of time to make his preparations. He needed a base and he needed transport. He changed dollars into pounds and bought himself a cassette player. His next stop was at a men's store on Piccadilly where he purchased shirts, pajamas, and underwear and a bag to carry them in. He climbed a floor and chose an overcoat. A cab took him to Lower Sloane Street where a car-rental firm honored his New Zealand license and supplied him with a blue Ford. He moved it four blocks to the offices of

WINTERBOTTOM & CAGE
SPECIALISTS IN SHORT RENTALS OF HIGH CLASS PROPERTIES

Drake told a clerk what he wanted. "A small house somewhere in Chelsea or Fulham."

The agent reached for a form. "May I have your name, please."

Drake passed the driving license across the desk. The agent copied the particulars.

"And your address, Mr. Muldoon?"

"Care of the Exbury Safe Deposit Company, S.W.1."

"How long would the let be for, Mr. Muldoon? There's a minimum of one month."

"That'll do," said Drake. "It's just about the period I had in mind."

A practiced glance gauged Drake's appearance. "How many bedrooms do you require?"

"I'm on my own," said Drake.

The agent opened a folder containing photographs of various properties. He turned the pages, giving the details as he went. A familiar name caught Drake's attention.

"Hold it," he said. "Did you say Savernake Mews?"

The agent caught fire. "That's one of our better lets, in fact. It has two bedrooms, living room, kitchen and dining area. The owner is in the south of France for a year. There are two floors and a small back garden."

Drake took a look at the photograph. The view of the rear of the house showed French doors leading out to the garden and beyond the garden an alleyway. He remembered the area well.

"How much?" he said.

The agent consulted his list. "That would be two hundred and fifty pounds a week, a month's rent payable in advance with a deposit of four hundred pounds. The deposit's returnable, of course. And we require the usual references."

Drake showed discolored teeth. "I'll take it," he said and counted out the money. "One thousand, four hundred. By the time you get my references from New Zealand I'll be out of the country."

Sight of the cash dissipated any doubt that the agent might have had. He scribbled a receipt and smiled anxiously.

"But are you sure you don't want to see the house first, Mr. Muldoon? You'll find everything shipshape, of course, but I can easily send someone around with you."

Drake shook his head and signed the lease. "As long as everything works I'll be satisfied. If not, you'll be hearing from me."

He left with the keys in his pocket. Driving was strange at first but he soon got the hang of it. Savernake Mews was a cobbled thoroughfare between King's Road and Fulham Road, bounded at each end by Victorian streets. Archways with stone lions guarded the entrances. Home for the young and fashionable had been converted from coachmen's houses. There were ten of them on each side of the mews. Drake's was the last on the right. He unlocked the front door.

A walnut-case clock ticked away in the white-painted hall. The house was warm. He peeped into the kitchen and what the agent had called the "dining-area." Everything he needed seemed to be there. He shut the door of the refrigerator and the motor whirred into action. He would have to buy food and drinks. A door opened into a large sitting room with bookcases, an oil portrait of a woman in her thirties, a desk, sofa, and television set. Heavy tweed curtains hung in the windows. Drake took a look outside. Beyond the French doors was a small paved garden with faded trompe l'oeil on one of the walls. A back door opened into the alleyway.

He climbed the stairs to the second story. Two small bedrooms were furnished to a woman's taste with pastel-hued sheets and pillows. The cane-headed bed exuded a faint smell of perfume. There were photographs of the same woman on a boat and riding horseback. He picked up the bedside phone and called Scotland Yard. Then he went out to do his shopping, leaving by way of the back door. The alleyway was too narrow to take a car and a good thirty yards away from the entrance to the mews. The house could not have been better designed for his needs.

At half-past twelve he was driving the Ford up Campden Hill, sure now at the controls. It was a residential neighborhood with no office buildings nearby and the bars and pubs were quiet at lunchtime. He left the car in a cul-de-sac and walked the rest of the way. Half a dozen vehicles were parked on the pub lot. Hackett's would be the red Cortina. Police car was written all over it. Drake waited in the outside lavatory for a while, still worried about being followed. He had always accepted the fact that the authorities would continue to show interest in his activities. He had been only part of the payoff ring and they knew it. Nevertheless they'd have to be discreet about their surveillance. Harassment was frowned upon. Their chief concern would be to find out if he had more money salted away. The trial judge had ranted on about dishonest men earning fortunes by betrayal of trust. The prosecution's assessment of the cash that had gone through Drake's hands had been fairly accurate. They had done their best to track it down, obtaining search warrants, sniffing through Mildred's legacy from her aunt, going into insurance policies and the deeds to the house. But they had missed the big prize and it made sense to assume that they'd know that they missed it.

On that score at least he was safe. No one knew about the Swiss bank account. Like the New Zealand passport and driving license it was his own production and as secret as his navel. The passport and license had been the property of a visitor to England killed in a car crash. Returned by the local police to Scotland Yard, they had vanished. Drake had switched the pictures himself. As Muldoon he was safe. There were no weak points in his scheme. He could handle drink and women and had all the money that he needed. More than that and most important of all, he had Hackett.

He used the side door into the pub. A bulldog snuffled in front of the fire. It was the kind of pub where plastic armorial shields hung on plywood paneling and the landlord wore a tattersall vest and a rose. It was over seven years since Drake had been there. A flight of stairs led up to a small restaurant where another fire was burning. A middle-aged woman tended the five tables.

Hackett was at a window table overlooking the parking lot. Drake took his weight off his feet, taking a good look at his one-time partner. Hackett had put on weight though much of it was concealed by good tailoring. He had always been a sharp dresser. His outfit today was a blue blazer with crested buttons, fine flannel slacks, and Italian loafers. There wasn't a thread of gray in the thick black hair that concealed his ears. Drake grinned. The bugger was still using dye, he decided. He was conscious of his own shabbiness in spite of the new

Burberry but then that had always been his image. He had always been the one who spilled soup on his clothes, trod hard on any bare feet in sight, and was ready to ram a stick of explosive down his grandmother's throat.

Hackett's practiced smile was totally false. "You look good, George!"

"Bullshit," said Drake and removed his overcoat. The waitress took their order and brought the drinks. Drake raised his glass, swallowing his first alcohol in six years.

Wariness showed in Hackett's carbon-colored eyes. "It's been a long time."

Drake spread his legs comfortably. "Longer for some than others. Though I have to admit you haven't exactly been wasting yours. Inspector to Chief Superintendent in less than eleven years. Not bad at all."

Hackett essayed a sneaky smile. "I had a good teacher."

"You're an asshole," said Drake, looking down at the food that the woman had brought. The steak-and-kidney pudding looked appetizing after the swill that he had been eating. Hackett inspected his cabbage doubtfully. "By the way," said Drake, "do you still see Mildred?"

"Mildred?" A look of surprise spread over Hackett's face. "Come on now, George," he said. "You know better than that."

Drake chewed on steadily to the end of the mouthful. "That's not gallant, Henry. My wife was good enough for you to screw for almost two years."

"Eighteen months," said Hackett. "And she's your ex-wife anyway. Look, that was a long time ago and you know it."

Drake loosed a creaky smile. "Things aren't always what they seem to be, Henry."

Hackett put down his knife and fork. "Just what is all this about, George? You call me out of the blue after, what is it — six, seven — years and ask me to meet you. First thing you want to do is talk about Mildred. We went through all that years ago."

"So we did," said Drake. He was enjoying his food. "I was

only kidding, Henry. I loathed the bitch. What I really want to talk about is you, my old friend Henry Hackett, head of the Drugs Squad. You see the point here is that I've done my time for my little caper. I can't be done twice for the same thing."

There was a hint of belligerence in Hackett's manner. "So?"

Drake hooked a finger inside his mouth and removed a shred of meat. "It isn't the same for you, Henry. The Statute of Limitations doesn't apply to conspiracy. You were into a whole lot of bad, bad things."

Hackett pushed his plate away. "You ask me to bring Raven's form sheet. So I do it out of friendship. And then what happens? First it's a woman I haven't set eyes on for years. Now stuff that I don't even understand."

"Patience," said Drake. "All will be revealed."

Hackett reached inside his blazer and threw an envelope on the table. "Here's what you asked for, George. I'm going to take a walk."

Drake shook his heavy head. "You're going nowhere. Why did you think I didn't pull the plug on you, Henry?"

Alarm leaked into Hackett's eyes. "What the hell are you talking about?"

"I had the proof," said Drake. "I still have it. It's all here. Dates, places, voices." He put the cassette player on the table.

Hackett stared at the machine as he might have at a cobra. "I don't believe you," he said finally.

"Then you're a bigger fool than I took you for." Drake switched on the player. The tinny voice that spoke was clearly Hackett's. Another voice joined in the conversation. The subject was sums of money to be paid, the terms and places for payment. Drake ran the tape forward. The voices changed but Hackett's was always there, the burden the same. When Hackett or Drake weren't actually speaking their names were being mentioned. The waitress was watching the table curiously.

"For crissakes," Hackett said in a low voice.

Drake switched off the machine.

"What are you trying to do to me, George?" Hackett demanded desperately.

Drake looked benevolent. "Explain the facts of life. By the way, they sent Kim Foo down to Winchester. We worked together on the garden party. He claims that you stitched him up, Henry. He says that you framed him because of the people in Hong Kong. He says that you've put everyone out of business except them."

Hackett was silent. "What's the matter?" Drake demanded. "Don't you like all this?"

Hackett shook his head. "You know as well as I do those little bastards will say anything. I got him bang to rights and that's God's truth. What are you trying to do, Henry? Crissakes, you and I go back a long way."

"That we do," said Drake. The taste of the Guinness was bitter. "And you've always been an asshole. I didn't keep my mouth shut because I liked you. You were my insurance. All those years I knew I had the means of yanking you out of whatever chair you were sitting in."

Hackett's face showed shock. "I'm straight," he insisted. "Your business scared the shit out of me. Kim Foo's a junkie and you know as well as I do they'll say anything."

Drake put the cassette in his hip pocket. "Not this one, Henry. He was scared and surrounded by foreign white devils. I was his friend and he confided in me. He told me about Mr. Hong. And he says you're still bent."

There was a degree of desperation in Hackett's denial. "He's lying."

"Not this time," said Drake. "You'll be taking backhanders on your deathbed. Not that it matters to me. I don't give a fuck what you do once I'm finished with you."

He opened the envelope Hackett had brought. Inside was a printout from the Central Police Computer. The sheet gave an outline of Raven's record while on the force. His passport number was on file, the numbers of his driving license and bank account. Drake signaled for the bill.

"You haven't eaten a thing," he said to Hackett.

"You're a real bastard," Hackett said in a low voice.

Drake grinned. "We both are, Henry. Is Raven still living on that houseboat?"

Hackett's face was dark with anger. "Look," said Drake. "I'm trying to make things easy for you."

"He comes and he goes," Hackett said reluctantly. "There's a woman in his life."

"That's more like it," said Drake." "It's going to be like old times, Henry. For a short time at least. I thought he lived alone."

Hackett's eyes were shifty. "He did. This is some Canadian he's been shacking up with, a photographer who lives in Paris. When she's not here, he used to be there."

Drake lit a cigar. "*Used* to?"

Hackett nodded. "There was a report through Interpol last year. Some Americans were printing phony stock outside Paris. People were killed and guess who bobs up in Switzerland, Captain Midnight himself! Not only that but the Swiss banks gave him over fifty grand in reward money. But the French didn't like it. He can't go back."

"What does he do with his time?" asked Drake.

Hackett moved his shoulders. "What did he ever do? Sticks his nose into other people's business."

Drake smiled his approval. "That's one thing you never did, Henry. Piss into the wind. You and I can do business." After years of being underdog he'd rolled over and was enjoying it.

"What kind of business?" Hackett's question was guarded.

Drake looked at his cigar judiciously. "Raven put me inside. If I hadn't played the white man you'd have been there with me. I'm going to knock him cold, Henry, and you're going to help me."

Apprehension vied with slyness now on Hackett's face. "I'll help you if I can, you know that. I don't have the same sort of attitudes that you do. You were my friend."

Drake picked up his change from the plate. "There's one

thing that you'd better keep firmly in mind. If anything strange happens to me . . . suppose I suddenly found myself back in the pokey, for example. That tape goes to the Commissioner. I'll leave the rest to your imagination."

Hackett's eyes were sliding off in every direction. "I don't pull that kind of shit, George. I never did and never will."

Drake hadn't smiled as much in a long while. "I want some scag, Henry. A good fat package of scag."

"*Scag?*" Hackett's grin was only partially successful. "Now you've got to be kidding. Where the hell do you expect me to lay my hands on that sort of stuff?"

Drake maintained his mood of false joviality. "That's an easy one, old man. You go straight back to the Yard and take the lift up to the sixth floor. Then you open up the Exhibit Room. If you don't score there use your Singapore connection. I don't care where you get it, just as long as you get it. O.K.?"

"You're out of your bloody mind," said Hackett. "Things have changed since you went away. People have been busted for doing the sort of thing that you're suggesting."

"I heard," said Drake. "But then they weren't as smart as you are. I want that heroin by six o'clock tomorrow night at the latest. And plenty of it. None of your matchbox scores."

Hackett glanced around nervously. "I'll need more time than that."

"Tomorrow night," Drake repeated. "I'm going to put you on a collar that'll make headlines, Henry. Six o'clock. I'll let you know where."

He stayed at the window, watching Hackett cross the parking lot to the red Cortina. Drake collected his overcoat and walked slowly to his car. He was pleased with the way things had gone. Halfway down Campden Hill he caught a glimpse of something red in the rearview mirror. He trod hard on the brake pedal and swerved to the curb. A truck passed but there was no sign of the red Cortina behind it.

Drake left the Ford outside his new home and strolled south

to King's Road. Chelsea had changed. He remembered the place when the sight of a black in African robes sent people running for their cameras. Now it was the turn of Japanese tourists with their square smiles and Canon compacts snapping the natives. He passed a group of teenagers, rouged and painted, their hair dyed like a parrot's plumage, nostrils and ears pierced with safety pins. He joined the throng in Safeway, an anonymous figure in a shabby blue suit and old homburg. He shopped, indifferent to price and quality, buying junk food and staples. His last purchase was a bottle of Bell's whisky. He stopped again on Fulham Road, buying a pair of Zip-Zoom binoculars coated for night viewing. Back at the mews, he entered the house through the garden. He saw nothing odd in the way he was behaving. Prudence was a habit of long standing.

It was already dark by the time he reached Forest Hill but the surroundings were familiar. Daylight would have shown a rash of follies built in the steeply sloping crescents and streets. Mock-Tudor villas, white and blue beach houses with chromed handrails and wraparound balconies, dinky little tile-and-timber homes. Now the street lights shone on trim hedges and patches of winter grass. Each house was sealed in respectability.

He drove to the top of the hill and stopped opposite the park gates. This was one of the highest points in south London. The vast city stretched away below, towers and pinnacles twinkling. There had been no room to build garages beside the houses on Oakwood Terrace, so they had been placed on the crest of the hill. He climbed out of the Ford and walked a remembered path. Twenty-two years he had lived on this street. Twenty-two years driving home most nights to a woman he progressively loathed. The fact that she had gone to bed with Hackett had nothing to do with it. He had disliked her from the first week of their marriage. He stood for a while outside the row of locked garages. The park had been closed for an hour and there was no one in sight. He bent in front

25

of one of the garage doors. The lock had not been changed. So far, so good. He put the key in and turned but it jammed. He tried to remove it, sweat breaking out on his neck. A dog barked nearby. He had a vision of Mildred walking up the hill, cranking her voice to a screech as she saw him. Suddenly the key slotted home and turned. He closed the door behind him and found the light switch.

The only thing that had changed was the car in front of him. He put his hand on the radiator of the TR6. It was cold. The Pirelli poster still hung on the wall, tattered and dirty. The workbench was littered with the home-tuning equipment used by a sports-car enthusiast. It was five minutes before he returned to the car. He had found a better hiding place than any safe-deposit box.

He ran into homebound traffic on the way back and it was after seven when he crossed Battersea Bridge. He parked on Old Church Street and stood there cracking the joints of his gloved fingers. The London smell was good, a November smell compounded of fuel fumes, the low-tide taint of the mudflats and the raw promise of fog. Traffic thundered along the embankment, long-haul trucks on their way west and north from the Channel ports, city workers and country shoppers.

Drake plodded on toward the river, thinking about Raven. There were few pedestrians. The flotilla of boats on the north shore were attached to the massive granite blocks that formed the river embankment. There were eleven of them. Upper Thames houseboats, converted barges, an old naval cutter, and a shrimp boat. None ever moved except up and down with the tide. Balks of timber, sodden bales of straw, and truck tires served as fenders.

The *Albatross* was the last in line. Lights shone in the cedarwood superstructure. Drake descended the slippery steps very carefully. Barbed wire festooned the door at the bottom making access without a key virtually impossible. Only the door and short gangway separated Drake from the deck. The sound of music drifted over the water. He took a good look at the lock on the door, climbed the steps again, and leaned over the parapet. The entrance to the boat was on the side farther away from the shore. He walked on for a hundred yards. A bend in the river gave him a better view of Raven's boat. He trained his night-glasses on the superstructure. The lens pierced the darkness with uncanny clarity. Suddenly the door opened. A tall girl with shoulder-length hair threw something over the side and closed the door again. Drake concentrated on the lock. He knew now the tools that he needed.

He drove crosstown to a shabby street behind King's Cross Station. Blackened brick walls hid the network of railroad tracks. The houses were mean, their fronts shored and boarded. Most bore notices condemning them as unfit for human habitation. He left the car and picked his way through broken glass and bricks. The house he was looking for was one of three that was still occupied. Age and structural defects made it lean out and away from its neighbors. A plumbline dropped from the roof would have landed six inches away from the street door.

Drake put his thumb on the bell. Except for the distant rattle of trains, the street was unnaturally quiet. The bell echoed shrilly. A second-story window was thrown up and the upper half of a man's body showed in the light. He had a sharp-angled face under a fringe of flat gray hair.

"Piss off!" the man shouted.

Drake rang the bell again. The whine developed into a snarl.

"'oo the bleedin' 'ell is it?"

Drake stepped backward, allowing the man to have a clear look at him.

"It's me, Albie."

The man leaned out further, to get a better fix on his visitor. Then he slammed the window down. Footsteps clattered down the stairs and the door was thrown open.

"Bleedin' 'ell, Mr. Drake!" said the man. "It give me quite a turn seein' you standin' dahn there."

"Well, let me in," said Drake. He'd known Albie Mitchell for the best part of sixteen years, a supplier of burglary tools to the fancy and big-time nark when betrayal was safe and rewarding. Drake followed Mitchell along a narrow hallway smelling of damp and poverty and up a flight of uncarpeted stairs. The scene changed on the second floor. The rooms might have been furnished by a garbage collector with a good route. The living-room carpet was heavily stained and had the insignia of a hotel woven into its fabric. There were office chairs on castors, Edwardian gas lamps, and a canteen table with a formica top. Only the gas fire and television set were modern. A myna eyed Drake from its cage. Mitchell drew his cardigan about him and closed the curtains.

"Yes, a real turn it give me," he repeated. He sought to frame his next remark delicately. "I thought you was still . . ."

"I was a good boy," said Drake, sitting down and unbuttoning his coat. "I behaved myself."

Mitchell's eyes and manner were uncertain. "Only goes to show. I mean — 'ere, 'ow about a drop of malt?"

"Nothing, thanks, Albie. You're wondering why I'm here, right?"

The front of Mitchell's cardigan was pitted with cigarette burns. "One thing's for sure, Mr. Drake. I'm glad to see you. You know that. You always treated me like a gennelman."

"I treated you like the scumbag you are," replied Drake. "A lot of people know you're a villain but I'm the only one who knows you're a nark as well." He stared around the room with distaste.

"I always played straight with you." Mitchell was whining again.

"That's because you knew what was good for you," Drake answered. "I don't like you. I don't trust you and I never did. You're going to give me some keys and get paid for it. One hundred and fifty pounds."

The sum brought a look of craftiness into Mitchell's eyes. "What sort of keys?"

Drake described the locks on Raven's boat. "There's a mortise and a couple of patent spring locks. They're called Fortress."

"Bastards," Mitchell said promptly. "They're worse than a Bramham or Ingersoll. There's no tolerance, see. No bleedin' room to maneuver."

"You've got the masters." It was a guess prompted by experience. Hidden somewhere in this house were the master keys to any commercial lock made.

"I'll 'ave to 'ave 'em back," said Mitchell.

"You'll get them back," said Drake and followed Mitchell down the stairs to a room at the back of the house.

Mitchell switched on a light and knelt in front of a safe cemented into the wall.

"'ave to keep everthing locked away. These fuckin' 'ooligans. They 'ave a go at me, they do, you know."

"The keys, Albie," Drake said impatiently. "I'm in a hurry."

Mitchell fumbled around inside the safe, unwilling for Drake to see its contents. He closed the door and stood up holding a leather wallet with the name Fortress stamped on it and a separate ring of slender keys.

"Them's the mortise skeletons," said Mitchell. "One of 'em's bound to do the trick but they ain't like no ordinary keys. You got to support the shank. There's no stop, see. You got to feel your way in."

Drake put the keys in his pocket. "I know what a skeleton key is, Albie." He opened the leather wallet. The keys inside were numbered one to five.

"It's got to be one of that series," said Mitchell. "But if you're rough with 'em, forget it. You'll jam the key in the lock and that's curtains. To tell the truth, Mr. Drake, I'm not too bleedin' 'appy about all this."

Drake counted out one hundred and fifty pounds. "Nobody asked you to be happy," he said and left.

The door closed behind him. He stood in the shadows a hundred yards away, looking back at the house. The lights went out as he watched.

3

THE NEW DAHL sound system had been built into the bookshelves. Raven was lying on the floor listening to records. His Klee was in its winter quarters over his desk where the light was best. The Skeaping bronze was new, a Camargue stallion standing on its hind legs. Raven was still spending the reward, two hundred and eighteen thousand Swiss francs after the canton had taken its tax cut. He had never expected the money or taken it seriously until a credit advice arrived from his bank. It was money to be spent extravagantly but there was a limit to his need of possessions and Kirstie had always resisted gifts.

He stretched out, reaching for the beaker of coffee. Kirstie was in the kitchen ironing. They had made love for the second time that morning with the desperation that always seemed to affect them before parting. She was taking an early flight back to Paris on the following day.

"It says here," he said, reading from the newspaper, "that we might get fog tomorrow."

She made no reply. He lowered the volume on the record player and tried again. "There could be fog tomorrow."

She came into the room carrying one of his shirts ironed to perfection. It was a chore that she loathed. Excelling at it marked her distaste.

"You're a strange man. I really think that you'd be glad if I didn't get away."

He rolled over, looking up at her. "Of course I'd be glad. What's so strange about that? You're a very attractive lady and I don't see enough of you."

"Attractive" was the right adjective, he decided, considering her. The sweater she was wearing matched her tawny hair. She had good bones, a generous mouth, and uncompromising eyes. She perched on the arm of the sofa, her long legs adjusting to the movement of the boat.

"Whose fault is it that you don't see enough of me?" she demanded. "I'm doing a job and Paris is my base. It's different for you. You can hang your hat wherever you please. You could come back to Paris with me tomorrow."

"That just is not true and you know it." He climbed up and opened a drawer in the painted desk. "Why don't we settle this once and for all?"

She watched him, wearing the slight frown that always went with her puzzlement.

"O.K.," he said. "There were four charges that could have been brought against me in France. Failure to report a serious crime to the forces of law and order, aiding and abetting dangerous criminals, fucking up in general. Right?"

"Do continue," she said. "I know how you hate interruptions when you're in full flow."

"Thank you," he said, bowing. "I was freed thanks to the whim of a certain Monsieur Papin, Prefect of Police. Maître Tain's estimate of my sentence if we went for trial was five years in jail and a heavy fine. That was assuming that we had the luck to land in front of a judge who was happy with the idea of foreigners interfering with the course of French justice."

"But instead, the hero's driven to Charles de Gaulle airport in a Citroën limousine with outriders." She seemed to find the idea genuinely amusing.

"That's right," he agreed. "And let me tell you the last thing those gentlemen said before they put me on the plane. They said 'Come back to France without first asking permission and we will break your balls!' Or words to that effect. Although you will have none of it, I found this very impressive."

She draped his shirt on the back of a chair. "That was over a year ago. They've forgotten your existence by now."

"Really?" He opened his passport at page three. There was an exit stamp bearing the device of the Sûreté Nationale. "See this? Well it shouldn't be there in the first place. No passports are stamped anymore between the U.K. and France. They're both members of the E.E.C. So why do you think it's there?"

She moved her shoulders. "I've no idea. Some sort of formality, I guess. Because of what had happened, maybe."

"Exactly," he said and pointed to a tiny mark in the center of the inked oblong. "This says all! The man at the controls doesn't even have to put your name through the computer. Nobody carrying this passport is going to get past a French immigration desk."

She changed her ground immediately. "Well, in any case you haven't even asked to be allowed back into France. It can't mean very much to you."

He returned the passport to the drawer. "You've got about as much sense of fair play as a scorpion. There's a very good reason why I haven't asked. I would have been refused. I've already established that much."

"How?"

"At diplomatic level."

"Nonsense," she said. "You don't know any diplomats."

"I pay taxes," he retorted. "And I know the telephone number of the Foreign Office."

Her expression was one of exasperation. "I don't know why you have to be so stubborn. A man has just gotten out of prison, someone you put inside. He swore to get even and what do you do, sit here and wait for him! You're crazy, that's what. We could be in Guadaloupe in eight hours. I'll trade in my ticket, call Paris, and buy a bikini. Come on, I dare you!"

He grinned. "I'm not supposed to be in the sun with my legs."

"You sonofabitch," she said. "What are you trying to do to me?"

"Show you how much I love you."

The declaration seemed to confuse her. She shook her head. "Why *should* I have to worry about you?"

"You're a natural worrier."

"I honestly don't know why I put up with you," she said. "Your sister's absolutely right. The only person whose feelings you're sensitive to is yourself."

"Terrific," he said. "That's all I needed, you to join forces with her." He had a sudden foreboding that he was reaching for something that was no longer there. As she had once said, nothing lasts forever.

"Well, you get what you see," he said. "I'll tell you what, I'll compromise. I'll call the Marbella Club and if it's sunny I'll book us a room. You can fly down from Paris and I'll meet you there."

"Don't forget your legs," she said.

"Name the day," he said.

She reflected. "I've got a job to do on Wednesday. How about Thursday?"

"You're on," he said. "Call me and tell me your flight."

They eyed one another for a couple of seconds. Then both grinned. "How about a movie?" he asked.

She moved spontaneously and kissed him on the cheek. "I'll get my coat."

4

THE RED PHONE buzzed on Hackett's desk. It was Berger. "You wanted me, sir?"

"Yes," said Hackett. "How does my diary look? I mean for the next couple of days."

Berger acted as a sort of secretary. His voice had the glottal stops of the native Cockney.

"You're supposed to be having a conference with the D.P.P.'s Department, eleven o'clock tomorrow. The Malhotra case."

The case he referred to concerned half a ton of cannabis resin and involved months of police work with look-alike Hindus making dummy runs. It could well be a tough one to win.

"Do you think you could handle the meeting?" asked Hackett.

"No problem. Is everything all right, Guv? You sound a bit under the weather."

The truth was that Hackett felt like a man on a lonely street with a razor held to his throat.

"A bit of a cold," he said. "Nothing to worry about. Let me know how you go with the Director of Public Prosecutions."

He put the phone down and started pacing the length of the room. The furnishings were standard. Metal files, a functional desk, a carpet the color of mud, and the usual calendar, courtesy of a firm of Birmingham handcuff makers. When his thoughts cleared he went to the phone again.

"Chris? It's Henry Hackett. Can we talk?"

"We can talk," said the voice. "And I know just what we're going to talk about. I hear from you twice a year and it's always the same bloody deal. What do you want this time?"

They had known one another for twenty-five years, served together in the East End, tough youngsters willing to cut corners in order to achieve the success that they both wanted.

"I want what I say kept locked up," said Hackett. "Just you and me, O.K.?"

"No, it's not O.K. I'm not making any blanket promises. What do you need?"

"I want a vehicle checked."

"You've got to be kidding! I'm in charge of traffic control. Stick your problem through the Iron Brain."

"I can't," said Hackett. "It's a delicate matter, Chris. I've got the numbers of a car that I'm fairly sure is rented. I want the address of the driver."

"Jesus Christ, Henry! What *is* this shit? You put the numbers through the computer and go to the rental firm. How did you get to be Chief Superintendent?"

"By getting people like you to help me out. You're not being very cooperative, Chris. I don't want this guy to know that he's being checked. Couldn't you put this number on the air and have one of your blokes call me as soon as there's a make? I mean, report to me personally?"

"Anything's possible," said the voice. "I've got twelve hundred men farting about in canteens when they're supposed to be looking for infringements of Her Majesty's Highway Code. They might as well be working for you."

"You can skip the sarcasm," said Hackett. "The numbers are Charley Zulu Warrior seven nine eight two. It's a blue Ford."

"No problem at all," said the other man. "I've only got twenty-six million vehicles on the roads. As a matter of interest, did you tell me why this isn't going through official channels?"

"No, I didn't," Hackett replied. "But I'll tell you now. It's because walls have ears and you're supposed to be a pal of mine. Are you going to do it or not?"

"I'm already doing it."

"Don't forget, whoever makes the sighting keeps the car

under surveillance and calls me personally. It's essential that the driver doesn't know that he's being tagged." Hackett gave his home and mobile numbers. "Thanks, Chris."

"Till death do us part. Is that the faint rustle of fifty-pound notes that I hear?"

"What you hear," said Hackett, "is a case of Scotch landing on your doorstep. I'll catch you later."

He went upstairs and used his key to the Drugs Squad Exhibit Room. He locked himself in, leaving the key in place so that he could not be disturbed. The room was lined with racks and thermostatically controlled. Typewritten cards tacked to the uprights gave the details of the exhibits. Hackett picked up one of the plastic bags. Attached to it was the label of the Metropolitan Police Forensic Laboratory. The chemical analysis identified the glittering white powder as heroin, No. 4 Chinese White, 87 percent pure, one and one quarter ounces in weight. Hackett replaced the heroin with a similar bag containing lactose and attached the Forensic Laboratory label. Analyses were never challenged. The bag didn't have to be produced until the December sittings of the Central Criminal Court and would be returned to Hackett for destruction in the prescribed manner.

He returned to his office, his mind still on Drake. Drake would have no hesitation in pulling the plug on him whenever he happened to feel like it. Everything would go. Job, pension, money. He'd come out of jail old, broke, and friendless. He did his best to get his mind off the subject by working. It was late afternoon when Drake phoned.

"Have you got it?"

"Yes," said Hackett.

"A quarter to five. The lobby of the Park Lane Hotel."

Hackett put one phone down and picked up another. "Chris? Have somebody in the area of the Park Lane Hotel at a quarter to five."

He parked on the narrow street behind the hotel. Drake was sitting in the lobby with a pot of tea in front of him, eating buttered scones. He wiped his greasy mouth and flapped a hand at Hackett. Hackett sat down and placed the brown-paper package on the table. Drake weighed it in his palm before putting it in his overcoat pocket.

"Good gear, is it, Henry?"

"It's Number Four Chinese White, eighty-seven percent pure. There's an ounce and a quarter there. All there was in the building. I'm sticking my neck way out here, George." He looked for a second cup but there was none.

"Where are you living these days?" asked Drake.

"I'm still at the same place. How about you? I mean I heard about the divorce. Mildred got the house, didn't she?"

Drake belched. "She got the house, Henry." He winked. "I don't think she was too pleased. It was mortgaged."

Hackett looked at his watch. "I can't stay long."

"I don't want you to stay long," said Drake. The two men considered one another. Drake broke the sudden silence. "Stay near a telephone, Henry. And when you get the word to move I want the *gantz*. I want cowboys and dogs and you leading the charge."

"It'll take a little time to set things up," said Hackett.

"You'll get time," promised Drake. He poured himself more tea and looked at it disparagingly. "I'm going to make you the hottest cop in the Met, Henry."

Hackett cleared his throat. "I keep my end of the bargain, how about you? I mean when do I get the tape?"

"All in good time, Henry," Drake said merrily. "All in good time."

Hackett caught a glimpse of himself in the mirror. He was getting a bit pouchy under the eyes. But Drake looked spryer than ever. Drake rose to his feet.

"Don't worry about seeing me to the door," he said. He left Hackett to pay for the tea and the scones.

No sooner was Hackett in the Cortina when the red button glowed on the dash. He lifted the receiver.

A voice sounded against the noise of traffic in the background. "P. C. Ellis, sir. I have vehicle Charley Zulu Warrior seven nine eight two in sight, a blue Ford being driven by a middle-aged man. He is proceeding west along Knightsbridge at approximately thirty miles an hour. Instruct, please. Out."

"Your vehicle?"

The traffic cop gave the number of his motorcycle. "I'm on my way," said Hackett. "Maintain observation and keep this line open!"

He barreled down the Piccadilly underpass, still talking to the patrolman. Drake was nearing South Kensington. Two minutes later he was going west along Fulham Road. Hackett was four cars behind the motorcycle cop when the blue Ford turned right into a mews. Hackett braked hard, speaking into the phone.

"Take a walk," he said, hung up, and hurried toward the mews. Hidden in the entrance, he was in time to see Drake entering the first house on the right. Hackett climbed back into his car. He had done enough for one day.

5

DRAKE was sitting on the south bank, between Grimaldi's Furniture Repository and the paper-wharf. There was only one other person around, a boy with a homemade rod and a package of sandwiches. He and Drake ignored one another in the way that fishermen do. It was a gray day. The water seemed to be without movement. Drake's rod was jammed between two stones, leaving his hands free. There was no bait on his hook. From time to time, he took the night-glasses from his lap and trained them on the *Albatross*. It was about four o'clock when Raven and the girl appeared on deck. A couple of minutes later, a gray Citroën turned left into the eastbound stream of traffic.

Drake gathered his things, climbed up to the car, and locked the rod and binoculars in the trunk. Then he walked across the bridge and into one of the pay phones. There was no reply from Raven's number. He descended the stone stairs and used Mitchell's keys. The spring lock at the end of the gangway opened at the second attempt. He walked along the deck, peeking through the curtains as he went. The second door took longer to open. His gloved fingers were clumsy as he tried to follow the locksmith's instructions. He finally made it and was standing in the long, warm room. It was almost the width of the boat and half as long with two deep sofas, a painted desk, and bronze statues of horses on the bookshelves. Drake's mouth set hard as he thought of the cell he'd occupied for almost six years. He walked into the kitchen and opened a window, giving himself a line of retreat should anyone surprise him. The converted barge pitched gently, sending the cups swinging on the dresser. A bathroom filled with plants divided into two bedrooms. Only one of them showed signs of being used. Raven's girl stared out from a silver frame on a side table. One whole wall was occupied by a step-in clothes closet. It was filled with Raven's suits and shoes. There was a Canadian passport and an Air France flight ticket to Paris on the dressing table. A half-packed suitcase lay open on the bed. Drake lifted out the thirty-five millimeter camera. The counter showed that the Contax was loaded. He opened the back and slipped a small packet of heroin under the strip of film stretched across the sprockets. Then he closed the camera again and put it back in the suitcase.

He was sweating as he walked back into the sitting room. He had been aboard the boat for eleven minutes but it seemed much longer. The tops of the curtains were covered with a matching valance. The curtains opened and closed electrically. He stood on the chair and pinned the second bag of heroin between the folds of the valance. Then he ran the curtains back and forth, looking at them from inside the room and from out on deck. There was no sign of the heroin. He shut the kitchen window and retraced his steps, making sure that no trace had been left of his visit. Five minutes later, he was back in his car. The boy had vanished. It was dark when he finally saw the lights of a car turning into the alleyway opposite Raven's boat. Drake focused his binoculars, following Raven and the girl along the deck. Raven stood aside to let her enter first. The curtains were left undrawn. Lights came on in the bedroom and sitting room. Raven was on the sofa, reading. There was no hint of alarm, no sudden dash for the phone. Just two people glad to be home and at peace. Then the curtains were drawn.

Drake drove back to the mews and called Hackett at home.

"Go," said Drake. "The woman's on a flight out of Heathrow tomorrow morning. Air France to Paris. There is only one. You'll find what you're looking for in the back of her camera. The rest of the stuff's pinned to the valance over the door leading out on deck. O.K.?"

"Got it," said Hackett. "Do I bust them together or separately?"

Drake thought for a moment. "Bust her at the airport and him on the boat. The more noise you make about this the better. I'll call you tomorrow morning and, Henry . . ."

"I'm listening," said Hackett.

"Make it good!"

6

Too much vodka the night before had wrecked Raven's timing. It was six-thirty when he woke and switched on the light. Kirstie was still asleep, a fan of hair hiding her face. Vodka was her drink, not his, and she knew nothing of the misery of hangovers. He slipped into his robe and went into the bathroom where he swallowed a couple of vitamin C tablets and ate a spoonful of honey. Then he started the percolator, drew the curtains, and unlocked the door leading out to the deck. Fog was creeping along the river on cats' feet and he could only just see the two bridges. He collected his newspaper from the box at the end of the gangway. There was no wind at all. The pennants and flags on the neighboring boats hung limp. Even the gulls were silent and still; the traffic was light along the embankment.

He shivered and stepped back into the warmth of the boat, shutting out the raw morning. The coffee was bubbling. He broke half a dozen eggs in a large bowl and started to beat them with a fork, scanning the newspaper as he did so. Fog was forecast for London. He scrambled his eggs, made toast, and called Air France. The girl on duty sounded as though she had already answered the same question too many times.

"No, sir, as far as we know all departing flights are taking off on schedule and there are no delays."

He carried the breakfast tray into the bedroom. The radio was playing quietly. He pressed a button, rolling the curtains back. Kirstie stirred in her nest of sheets and blankets, making a face as she looked out through the window. She slept naked, a gold bear dangling between her breasts. He threw his pajama top at the bed and she struggled into the pale blue jacket. He removed her clothes from the chaise longue and sat down beside her. Suddenly he had no appetite. All he wanted was coffee.

"I called Heathrow," he said. "There's no fog out there. Everything's running on schedule."

She forked egg into her mouth, her face unconcerned. "I know it. They just said so on the radio. You look terrible."

"I feel terrible," he admitted. "That vodka's a killer. I should stick to Scotch. Do you want me to drive you to the airport?"

She shook her head, glancing at the windows again. "No, it'll take forever to get out of town. You can drop me off at Sloane Square Underground."

He showered and shaved and put on jeans and sneakers and the mackinaw she had sent from Canada. By the time he had cleared the breakfast things Kirstie was dressed. She was wearing the outfit she usually wore for traveling, sweater, cords, and an old green loden cloth coat. Her hair was tied behind her head, her face freshly washed. Without makeup she looked about eighteen.

"I'll call you tonight and let you know about Marbella," he said.

She put her suitcase down and went through her purse, checking her passport and flight ticket.

"I guess we'd better make a move," she said, looking up at him.

The fog was a dirty shroud of cotton obscuring the flotilla of boats. They crossed the embankment to the parked Citroën. Raven drove slowly though he could have negotiated the journey blindfolded. There was little traffic. He pulled up outside the Underground station and reached across to open the door for her. As always he was reluctant to let her go.

"Call me if your plane's delayed," he said. "I'll come out and keep you company."

"Sure," she answered and leaned in through the open window, transferring a kiss from her lips to his with the tips of her fingers. "I've got a good man and I don't treat him right."

She had gone before he had the chance to read the expression in her eyes. He drove home, depression already setting in. The weather did nothing to help his mood. He switched on the electric blanket and climbed back into bed. He was asleep in five minutes.

A loud crash jerked him back into consciousness. A second crash reverberated through the hull. He grabbed his pants and ran through to the sitting room. The deck was crowded with cops. Plainclothesmen, German shepherd dogs with their handlers. Shock and anger invaded his mind as he saw the broken door at the end of the gangway. The leader of the invaders was a burly well-dressed man with thick black hair and a fleshy nose. A younger and taller man stood at his shoulder hefting a fireman's ax. His arm lifted and the blade bit into the frame of the door. His second blow took the door off its hinges.

The two men stepped in, kicking aside splintered wood and broken glass. Other men poured in behind them, the dog handlers restraining their charges on heavy choke-chains.

Anger made Raven's voice unsteady. "Just what the hell do you think you're doing!"

The burly man flashed a warrant card in a plastic case. He brought his face close to Raven's.

"Detective Chief Superintendent Hackett. I've got a warrant to search these premises!"

The boat had suddenly overflowed. Police were everywhere, in the bedrooms, kitchen, and bathroom.

"Search them for what?" Raven demanded.

"Drugs."

Raven shook his head slowly. There was a bundle of home-grown grass with the herbs in the kitchen. With a sense of unreality, he understood that he was about to be busted for smoking a joint.

"I just don't believe it," he said. "What do you think this is, some sort of carnival?"

Hackett's hand caught Raven off balance and sent him staggering backward. Someone threw him the rest of his clothes. He picked himself up and dressed.

"You talk too much," said Hackett.

A couple of men on deck cut off any chance of escape. Hackett's grin widened as he climbed up on a chair. He reached among the folds of the valance and stepped down holding up a plastic bag filled with white powder. Looking at it, Raven realized what was happening to him. Hackett moistened the tip of his index finger and tasted the powder. The look on his face was close to admiration.

"Jesus Christ!" he said, turning to the sandy-haired man at the desk. "This stuff is fucking dynamite!"

His aide nodded. "Chinese White by the color."

Hackett returned his attention to Raven. "I thought you were supposed to be an intelligent man. You don't act like one. You've been had, dasher. The Chinaman's a nark."

The sandy-haired man was rifling through Raven's desk. "This is Detective-Sergeant Meade," said Hackett. Raven's mouth was completely dry. "The Chinaman's made a statement," said Hackett. "He says he sold you this dope last week. He says he's been supplying you with scag for the last two years."

"I want to make a phone call," said Raven.

"You don't need a phone call," said Hackett. "What you need is a fucking miracle. On your feet, you're nicked and you're cautioned!"

Raven came off the sofa. The thinking part of his brain was stunned, only the instincts of a hunted animal were working. Hackett was close to him as they moved out on deck. Other men closed in behind and in front. The Superintendent spoke over his shoulder.

"Get somebody to fix those doors and move the Citroën out of the alley."

44

Raven sucked in a long deep breath as they moved toward the gangway. It was now or never. He jumped up on the bulwark, holding his pose for a split second before diving. He reached out as far as he could with his eyes shut tight. The last thing he heard before hitting the water was Hackett's shout.

Raven was beneath the surface now, arms flailing in a desperate breast stroke. Bursting lungs finally forced him up. The lights along the embankment were tenuous, their power and definition destroyed by the fog. He was some twenty yards downstream from the *Albatross*. Men were shouting to one another but it was impossible to see where they were.

Lights were burning dimly on some of the other boats and people had come out on deck. He could hear his neighbor's Great Dane barking, the sound deeper than that of the police dogs. Police sirens wailed in the distance. He struck out again, swimming in an arc that was designed to take him back toward the flotilla of boats. The water tasted of mud and the movements of his calf muscles were agony. Fog had draped itself over the river, muffling sound, its clammy presence shrouding the buildings and bridges. Raven turned over on his back, making slow headway against the current. He could hear a police whistle blowing, dogs barking, men shouting.

He used his hands and feet in a kind of paddle that carried him toward the boats. Now he could hear the creak of timber, the straining of hulls, the slapping sound of water. Then his fingers touched the side of a boat. He worked his way along, legs scraping against the barnacles. It was impossible to read the name of the boat on the stern but he recognized it by its smell. The owner was a sixty-year-old writer whose work was brilliant and unsalable, a man who offered little to the world and who demanded still less from it.

A length of rope dangled from a rail overhead. Raven grabbed it and hauled himself up to collapse on the deck of the shrimp boat, cold and exhausted. Water streamed from his clothes. His own boat was thirty yards away but six feet was as far as he could see. He pulled himself together and tried the hatch. It was unlocked. Greg Vanders always said that a succession of girlfriends and wives had left him with nothing worth stealing except his work and nobody wanted that.

Raven divested himself of his shirt, wrung it out, and used it to mop the deck where he had been lying. He climbed down the ladder, lowering the hatch as he went. The sound of pursuit gradually dwindled and he rammed the bolts home. He groped his way into the darkness, calling Vanders' name softly. There was no answer. He knew the boat well and felt along the wall until he reached Vanders' sleeping quarters. There was enough light to give form to some of the objects around him. He undressed and dropped his discarded clothing into the bilge. All he retained were his waterproof watch and the few pounds that were in his pockets. He found Vanders' bureau and a pair of pants and a sweater that fitted him. He kept his sneakers. Vanders' feet were smaller than his.

Suddenly the cabin brightened. A searchlight swept across the portholes as a police car was slowly driven along the Embankment. A voice bawled through a loudspeaker.

"All right, people! Everybody back to your boats, please! The show's over, let's move it out of there!"

The light swept past again, this time coming from the opposite direction. Raven stood at the bottom of the ladder, making his breathing as shallow as possible. The only way out was through the hatch. The portholes were too small to crawl through. He climbed a few rungs and raised the hatch. He could hear men's voices on the deck of the neighboring boat. He climbed up on deck and lowered the hatch very gently. Then he stood on the stern, waiting. Somebody coughed close at hand. A flashlight showed dimly through the fog. Raven stepped over the low bulwark, grabbed the rope, and hung there. If they discovered him he would have to drop. Hunger, pain, Kirstie, were pushed to the back of his consciousness. His senses were honed, his mind alert, everything except the need to survive was forgotten. The boat listed slightly as some-body stepped aboard. Raven could hear the hatch being lifted, feet going down the ladder. His arms were beginning to tire. The man was climbing the ladder now. When he reached the deck, he shouted.

"There's nothing here, Guv!"

Hackett's muffled answer floated back. "Let it go, Tim. The bastard's still in the water!"

The boat tipped again as the man stepped ashore. Raven stayed where he was, the rope swaying, imagining a line of police cars drawn up along the embankment, men and dogs frozen in nervous silence, a battery of searchlights ready to be switched on as soon as he appeared. He pulled himself up painfully and lowered the hatch behind him. He lay down on Vanders' bunk, considering his position. He'd been framed and Drake's trademark showed in the scope and ingenuity of the plan. What didn't add up was the reason for Hackett's involve-ment. For the head of the Drugs Squad to lend himself to such a scheme suggested extreme pressure of one kind or another. The one sure thing was that Hackett wouldn't be bluffing about his Chinaman. A man in Hackett's position could always lay his hands on someone ready to perjure himself. The raid had been made legally, the heroin found in front of witnesses. This was going to be no lightweight affair. They were hitting him with everything that they had. A sudden thought came to mind. He reached for the drawer by the bunk. Inside was Vanders' old Smith and Wesson. All five chambers were load-ed. Raven put it under the pillow. When he next looked at his watch it was ten minutes past five. He must have slept. It was already dark outside and strangely quiet. He wrote a note to Vanders explaining about the clothes but saying nothing about taking the gun. Vanders would know that soon enough.

Raven lifted the phone on the chest. He dialed and spoke with his hand cupped over the mouthpiece.

"Don't ask questions. Meet me at Kim's. Leave now."

He climbed the ladder, taking an old mackintosh that was

hanging on the back of the door. He raised the hatch a couple of inches. The lights along the embankment looked like fishbowls suspended in the watery fog. A shaky gangway connected Vanders' boat with the landing stage. Raven crossed it. The lower stone steps were underwater. He crept up toward the crawling traffic. Car headlights barely pierced the gloom. He crossed the embankment and started walking east. His car had been removed but there were no shouts or police whistles, no hands seeking to detain him. The *Albatross* was in darkness.

Visibility improved as he put distance between himself and the river. People still circulated carefully, some with flashlights passing each other with guarded mistrust. He boarded the Underground at Sloane Square and left the train at Aldgate. Red dragons glowered at one another in the window of a restaurant 300 yards away. A CLOSED sign hung in the door. Raven rang the bell. A Chinese youth opened the door for him. The youth nodded toward the end of the room and vanished. Raven walked past a varnished bamboo bar, soapstone figures, and dragons and devils.

Jerry Soo was drinking Coke at a table, a squat forty-year-old with short blue-black hair and gold teeth. He was wearing a track suit overprinted with the emblem of the Metropolitan Police Judo Club and basketball sneakers. The corner of his mouth was spiked with a toothpick. Raven pulled up a chair. Soo always referred to the owner of the restaurant as family, a claim that Raven found hard to understand. Soo had been found, seven weeks old, in a vegetable basket and raised by the staff of the Hong Kong Methodist Memorial Hospital. The fact remained that Soo and the restaurant owner treated one another with the grave respect displayed by close relatives in their homeland.

Raven took a swig of Soo's Coke and told all. His friend listened impassively, switching the toothpick from one side of his mouth to the other. Their friendship went back eighteen years to the Detectives Training School at Hendon. It was a friendship without limits. Raven had read once that a true friend was a man you could trust with your liberty, your woman, and your money. Soo had kept faith on all scores.

Soo looked Raven over. "So where did you get the clothes?"

"From the boat. This writer I know. It has to be Drake, Jerry."

Soo's boot-button eyes were bright. "Yep. Hackett used to be Drake's right-hand man. It wouldn't be coincidence."

"You're damn right it isn't coincidence." Telling his story had made Raven even more aware of the danger he was in. "Is there any way you could find out where Drake is living?"

"Why?"

Raven's tone sharpened. "Because I want to know."

Soo shook his head. "I already tried. In fact I checked as soon as I saw his name on the list. I don't like it, John. Have you been in touch with Patrick yet?"

"No," said Raven. "I thought his phone might be bugged."

"So could mine," Soo said promptly. "In fact I'd say that I'd be first on the list." He thought for a moment. "O.K., let's see what we've got here. Number one, they've found heroin on your boat and they've gone in with a search warrant. That means Hackett must have given some sort of grounds for the warrant. Number two, they've got a witness who says that he sold dope to you. Number three, when you're arrested, you go over the side of the boat. Agreed?"

Raven nodded. "So?"

"Level-headed people are going to ask themselves why an innocent man would run?"

"Is that just rhetoric," Raven demanded, "or am I supposed to answer it?"

Soo threw his toothpick in the ashtray. Then he walked to the refrigerator behind the bar, took out another can of Coke and popped the top. He came back to the table wearing a mustache of brown foam.

"I've just remembered something that's written on a wall in

one of the johns at the Yard," he said. "It seems that nobody seems to want to clear it off. It says 'the only piece of shit you can't get rid of is Henry Hackett.' I don't know too much about the guy but I wouldn't underestimate him."

"*Underestimate* him?" Raven's voice was almost shocked. "I'm in no position to underestimate anyone, Jerry. I don't even know where I'm going to put my head down tonight."

"You want to know what I think?" Soo said.

"What?"

Both men seemed to decide on a period of silence. It was Soo who broke it.

"I think you should turn yourself in."

Raven did his best to keep the bitterness out of his voice. "Great advice. Thanks."

Soo grinned. "But I don't expect you to do it. Come on, let's go."

"Go where?" Raven demanded.

"To Louise's studio. She's only had it a month. Nobody knows about it except her, the landlord, and me."

Soo rattled a key on the Coke can and the youth appeared. Soo spoke a few words in Cantonese. The youth replied. Soo aimed his grin at Raven.

"He says he's honored by the visit of his uncle. That's you."

Raven waited in the battered Volkswagen while Soo shopped along Cable Street. He came back with provisions, blankets, and a sleeping bag. He threw these on the back seat and settled himself behind the wheel. It took them an hour to cover six miles. Soo drove with both windows down and his nose pressed against the windshield. The fog drifted from street to street and what traffic there was proceeded with caution. Soo finally stopped the Volkswagen with its headlights nuzzling a tall brick wall.

He cut the lights and nodded at a door in the wall. "Home," he said simply.

Raven followed, carrying the things Soo had bought. He

knew roughly where he was. It was an area just south of the river and scheduled for redevelopment. He was no more than a couple of miles from his boat.

There was enough light to see a brick chapel and a row of six studios built side by side. Soo flicked a thumb at the chapel.

"The Moravian Brethren. They won't bother you. There's only one service a week."

He opened the door to one of the studios and switched on the lights. The curtains were already drawn. Soo felt the radiators and flushed the cistern in the lavatory. He offered his angled smile again.

"It's not the Savoy but it's safe."

The windows were double-glazed, the walls and doors soundproofed. This was where Louise Soo practiced her cello. The rugs, mats, and pictures came from her home in Taiwan. Beanbags were scattered over the floor. There was only one room, a kitchen-alcove, and lavatory. Soo took a radio out of a closet.

"For God's sake stop walking up and down," he remonstrated. "You're making me nervous. Sit down somewhere."

Raven lowered himself on the music stool. "That's better," said Soo. "Now here's how it works. The other five tenants are artists. At this time of the year the light's no good after four o'clock. They tend to go home early but don't bank on it. The one important thing is that no one's supposed to sleep here. The lease says tenants have to be off the premises by six o'clock at night."

"And the priest?"

"The pastor," Soo replied. "He's the landlord. He lives in Richmond but he spends a lot of his time in the pub next door. He's called Murdoch and he's eight feet tall."

"Did you say Moravian Brethren?" asked Raven.

"That's right," said Soo. "There are four hundred thousand of them, mostly Jamaicans. And don't touch the curtains. People are used to seeing them closed. Louise likes privacy when she practices."

Soo watched, his face impassive, as Raven took the revolver from his mac pocket.

"Since you're not going to turn yourself in," said Soo, "maybe you'll give me some idea of what you have in mind? That's assuming that you know."

Raven managed a half-smile. "I'll think of something. Though right now I don't seem to be doing too well."

Soo picked up the revolver. "And this? What do you intend to do with this thing?"

Raven shrugged. "I'm not too sure. But I need all the help I can get."

"That's not help, that's trouble," said Soo. "Look, John, a gun isn't going to solve your problem."

"It just might," Raven said obstinately. "If I can find Drake it might well solve the problem."

Soo shook his head. "I stopped trying to reason with you seventeen years ago. At least let me get in touch with Patrick. As your lawyer he ought to know what's going on."

"Tell him," said Raven. "Just don't let him know where I am. That way his conscience is clear. Look, Jerry. Try to understand my position. If I surrender, I'm finished. You and I both know that I've been framed and we know who's framed me. But just try to prove any of it. I'm the one who has to find the proof."

Soo continued to stare. "What's the matter?" Raven demanded. "You're looking at me as though I'm doomed."

"You ought to have gone when I told you," Soo said sadly. "I knew that bastard meant trouble the moment I saw his name on the list."

"O.K.! You knew it, Kirstie knew it, I didn't listen. But I'm the one who's involved," said Raven.

"We're all involved," answered Soo.

Raven tried to explain. "I don't *want* you involved, Jerry! O.K., a place to sleep, a little help if you can but this is something that I have to do by myself. Friends or not, there's nobody who can go where I have to go."

"Have you thought about Kirstie?" Soo asked quietly.

A clock chimed outside in the chapel. "I've thought about Kirstie," Raven said steadily. "She'd worry herself sick if she knew what had happened. Not only that, there's nothing she can do to help."

"Wrong," said Soo. "The woman loves you. She has the right to know what has happened."

The two men glanced at the phone as if by common design. "You want me to call her?" asked Soo. Raven nodded. Soo found another toothpick in the recesses of his track suit and dialed. "No answer," he said, looking across the room. "She must be out."

Raven looked at his watch. It was twenty minutes past eight. He tried to remember if there was an hour's difference in time between Paris and London.

"Yes," he said. "She has to be out."

Soo dragged the sleeping bag and blankets nearer the radiator. The studio apartment was warm by now.

"I think I'd better get back to the factory. There's a guy on the Drugs Squad who comes to my judo class. I'll try to find out what's going on. Don't worry, I'll be discreet. I'll call you back later. O.K.?"

"O.K." Raven hesitated. "You think I'm doing the wrong thing, don't you, Jerry?"

Soo's scalp was the color of parchment under the light. "I've rarely known you do the right thing but then it always seems to work for you. I just hope that it doesn't backfire this time."

He lifted a hand, winked, and was gone. Raven heard the stutter of the departing Volkswagen and the studio was suddenly quiet. He switched on the radio and tuned in to a news station. There were reports of traffic disasters due to the fog, pileups and rear-end collisions. Better weather was forecast. A Dorset woman had found a Jacobean chafing dish in her hen-house. A bullion van had been robbed. There was no mention of a police raid upon a Chelsea houseboat. He turned off the radio and started unpacking the provisions.

7

HACKETT drove the Cortina down the ramp and climbed the stairs leading from the subterranean garage to the police station. The station officer glanced across from his desk.

"Do you know where Meade is?" asked Hackett. "Detective-Sergeant Meade?"

The sergeant jerked his thumb at the ceiling and removed a large fountain pen from between his teeth.

"Yon woman's been making a nuisance of herself," he said in a rich Aberdonian accent.

"Doing what?" Hackett demanded.

The sergeant's smile released the odor of peppermints. "A policeman's life is no one for them with finer feelings. Miss Macfarlane doesnae think much of us. She kept asking to make her phone call."

"And?"

"That's what she did," said the sergeant. "She's entitled to it. She's been charged and she's had Form A."

Hackett controlled his temper. "You're got no business letting a prisoner make a phone call without as much as asking C.I.D."

The sergeant leaned his arms on the desk. He was very sure of himself. "You run your case, Superintendent. I run the station. Yon girl has the right to communicate with a lawyer or member of the family."

"Who did she call?" asked Hackett. There was no point in getting involved in an argument.

The sergeant handed him a slip of paper. On it was written the name Patrick O'Callaghan with an address on Upper

Berkeley Street. Hackett lifted the heavy bunch of keys from the desk.

"I'm taking her up to the Interview Room."

He unlocked the gate at the end of the corridor. Kirstie Macfarlane was the only prisoner in the cells. She was huddled on the bench in her loden cloth coat. The heating didn't seem to extend this far.

"O.K.," said Hackett. "Grab your things. We're going upstairs."

She looked at him blankly. "What for?"

"A talk," he said smiling.

The movement she made was half-shrug, half-shiver. "I've been through all that once. I don't want to talk anymore."

"On your feet," he ordered. "This is different."

He waited as she picked up her purse. She looked him full in the face as she passed through the doorway. He had seen her for the first time a couple of hours after they had brought her from Heathrow. One of her escorts claimed that she had almost broken down in the car but there was no sign now of any weakness. Hackett took her up to the second floor and left her in the Interview Room with a uniformed W.P.C. He found Meade typing with four fingers, his hair the color of wet sand under the hundred-watt lamp.

"Did you know that she made a phone call?" Hackett demanded.

Meade swung his chair around. "The desk sergeant told me. She was trying to reach a lawyer. He called back half an hour ago, wanting to know what she'd been charged with."

"And you told him?" said Hackett. There was a gap between Meade's front teeth. Combined with flat, lobeless ears it gave him a look of boyish belligerence.

"I told him," said Meade. "And he wanted to know who was in charge of the case. I told him that too."

"I've got her in the Interview Room," said Hackett. "Come in there with me. I'll do the talking."

It was warmer in the Interview Room. Kirstie had taken off her coat and was sitting at the table, smoking. Hackett and Meade joined her, leaving the W.P.C. standing near the half-open door.

"Right," said Hackett. "This is just a chat to clear up a few points, Kirstie. The first thing I want you to know is that I'm trying to help you."

"Really?" she said. "I'd prefer to be called Miss Macfarlane, Superintendent. I'm not in the habit of being addressed by my first name by people I don't know."

Hackett's smile was lopsided. "You've got yourself involved in something very stupid and sooner or later you're going to have to face the fact."

She took a long drag on her cigarette, closed her eyes, and then opened them again.

"I've done nothing wrong, Mr. Hackett. I am involved in nothing."

Meade assumed a broad grin. "That's silly," said Hackett. "And I can see that you're not used to telling lies. It's written all over your face. The plain truth is that you've been used, young lady. You've been left holding the bag. And I wouldn't look to Raven for help."

"You're wasting your time," she said steadily.

His fingers stroked his meaty nose. "I want to help you."

"That's the third time that you've said it," she answered. "But I don't believe you."

"Do you want to get us some coffee?" he asked, turning to Meade. He told the W.P.C. to stand outside the door. Once alone with Kirstie, he leaned forward, speaking quietly and persuasively. "Look, you're living with a known dealer in drugs. Heroin was found hidden in your camera. Are you trying to tell me that there's an innocent explanation for all this?"

She used his matches to light another cigarette. "I know as much about it as you do, possibly less. I'm not a user of drugs. I've never dealt in drugs. And the first time in my life that I saw heroin was at Heathrow this morning."

She appeared quite sure of herself. He was beginning to dislike her in a way that was entirely personal.

"I've been at this game over twenty-five years," he said. "And one thing it does is give you a feel about people. Yet I can't make you out, know what I mean?"

She considered him through a curl of smoke. "No, I do not know what you mean. There's nothing enigmatic about me. I live with John Raven by choice. He is *not* a drugs dealer. I have my own apartment in Paris where I work as a free-lance photographer."

He leaned again, behind a pointing finger. "That camera was opened in your presence. Three people were there besides yourself. Two police officers and a Customs and Excise official."

She moved her head in acknowledgment. "I know it. But I'm still not responsible for the heroin being there."

He changed tack sharply. "Your boyfriend has disappeared. He vanished as soon as he heard that you'd been arrested."

"I don't believe it," she said. "You're lying."

He shook his head. "We went to the boat to interrogate him. He escaped. The thing is, if you're telling the truth it means that someone else put that dope in your camera. The question is who?"

A flicker of doubt crossed her face. "I've already tried to explain, Mr. Hackett. I just do not know. The last time I used that particular camera was four days ago in Paris."

He grinned. "Then why bring it with you?"

She gathered a breath then let it go. "For God's sake, I'm a professional photographer!"

He took a piece of paper from his blazer pocket. "Wherever he's gone, your boyfriend won't be in France, will he?"

She shrugged, her eyes wary. "I've got a Telex message here," Hackett continued. "It's from the Sûreté Nationale. It says that Raven was deported from France."

"Not true," she said calmly.

Meade was back, carrying three cartons of coffee. Hackett gave one to Kirstie.

"What I've said here is strictly off the record. You seem to me like a nice girl and I don't want to see you hurt. I want you to go back to your cell and ask yourself a few questions. Ask yourself who could have planted that dope in your camera and ask yourself why. Let me make a suggestion. It could have been someone who wanted that heroin outside the country and didn't want to take the chance of carrying it himself."

She looked at him with open distaste. "I've no idea how good a detective you are but you're a very poor judge of character."

He smiled. "If you can think where your boyfriend's likely to be, it could save you a lot of heartache. I'll be available any time you want to talk to me."

She stubbed out her cigarette with one quick gesture. "I'd like to make a telephone call, please."

"You get one call and you've already had it," he said.

She gave him stare for stare. He shrugged. "O.K." He took her into the office that the Drugs Squad was using. He picked up the phone. "What's the number?"

He recognized it as soon as she spoke. It was the number of Raven's boat. It started to ring and he passed the telephone to her, smiling. She put the phone down after a couple of minutes. Her head was still held high.

"I'd like to go back to my cell if you please."

•

It was six o'clock in the evening. Most of the fog had lifted. Hackett could see Savernake Mews. He had been in the neighborhood for three quarters of an hour, circling the block, watching both entrances to the mews. His car was parked 300 yards away, on a parking lot in front of an apartment building. It was another twenty minutes before Drake's blue Ford was driven under the archway. Hackett hurried after it. By the time he reached the cobblestones, the lights were on upstairs in Drake's house. The car had been left out front. Shielded by it, Hackett inspected the locks on Drake's front door. Then he walked around to the rear of the house. An alleyway six feet wide ran parallel with the mews. He looked through the back door keyhole. Drake's silhouette showed at an upstairs window.

Hackett returned to his car. He remembered Drake's arrest only too well, the days and nights that had followed when every summons to a phone had been a threat. He hadn't relaxed until Drake's conviction, grateful that he had been let off the hook yet without knowing why. He should have had more sense. Drake had never given anyone a break, nor would he now. The moment that Hackett had served his purpose he would be dumped. There was only one sure way that he could protect himself.

*

Back at Chelsea police station, he found Meade still at his typing. Hackett hung his overcoat on the back of the door. The room that had been placed at their disposal had two windows overlooking the exercise yard. The linoleum was cracked, the grate filled with waste paper. It was a room that was normally used for storage and it looked and smelled like it.

Meade stretched elaborately. "There's someone been trying to reach you, Guv. Communications relayed the call. He says it's important but he won't give a name or a number."

Hackett showed no interest but he knew who the caller was. He glanced through the notes relating to Raven's arrest and escape. He signed the four pages and returned them to Meade. His aide was an odd mixture of ambition and honesty. As far as Hackett knew, Meade had never offered a favor to a prisoner nor had he asked for one. Everything was done according to the rule book. There was an implicit moral attitude about it and Hackett mistrusted all moral attitudes. As far as he was concerned there was only one deterrent, fear. The rest was bullshit. Meade lived at home, played rugby football and dated a girl who worked in a picture gallery. Hackett reasoned that the dice had already rolled for the younger man and nothing there was going to change.

Hackett kicked the door shut. He would be glad to be back in his own office with its aura of respect and authority. Yet with the threat of the tape, the prospect carried its own anxiety.

"What happened about the bug on O'Callaghan's phone?"

Meade put his notebook away. He copied Hackett's style as far as his means allowed. His tan trenchcoat with its buckles and straps was a cheaper version of a coat that the Chief Superintendent wore.

"Nothing," said Meade. "It seems that there's a Home Office directive about bugging members of the legal profession."

The news reaffirmed Hackett's own suspicions but he still asked the question.

"Who told you that?"

"Vinson," said Meade. "Apparently if you want to tap a lawyer's phone, authority has to come from the Minister himself. And to make it stick you have to catch the guy in bed with a known villain."

"Vinson's a prick," said Hackett.

Meade offered his gap-toothed grin. "Fair enough but he also happens to be Executive Assistant Commissioner."

Hackett propped his feet against the fireplace. There were limits to what he could say to Meade. The drive that made his aide ambitious also made him cautious.

"I was talking to one of the local C.I.D.," said Meade. "Someone who knows O'Callaghan well. He's rubbed their nose in it quite a few times."

Hackett was unimpressed. "Let's see how he goes with this one."

"They say he's got friends in high places," Meade went on.

Hackett turned his head. "Fuck O'Callaghan, Tim. I want to know where you think Raven is."

It was a while before Meade committed himself. "Well, one thing's for sure. He's not going far without help."

"He'll get help," said Hackett. "And that too is for sure. He's another one with friends."

Meade popped a stick of gum in his mouth. He had recently given up smoking.

"The thing I find strange, Guv, is the way he suddenly comes on the scene. I mean as a dealer. I tracked back a bit in the files. There's no mention of him anywhere and none of the regulars ever even heard of him."

"That's where he's smart," said Hackett. "All these other assholes make themselves known."

"What about motive?" Meade's eyes were curious. "He's supposed to have all the money he needs. You saw that boat and his car must have cost seven or eight grand."

"Wrong," said Hackett. "Nobody has all the money he needs."

Meade thought about it. "Well, maybe you're right, Guv. It just seems to me to be out of character. Do you really think that he planted that stuff in her camera?"

Hackett grinned. "When I'm sure I'm never certain, Tim. Our job's to find out the truth. The woman lives in Paris, right? She's got a legitimate reason for coming and going. They could be in it together. The fact remains that both had dope. We start from there."

Some of the doubt left Meade's face. "You could cut that stuff ten times and still make a fortune on the street."

Hackett nodded. The heroin taken from Raven and the girl would be produced in evidence and sent to Forensic for the second time for analysis. The thought gave him a certain amount of amusement.

Meade yawned again. "Are you putting Lee Fook in the box tomorrow?"

Hackett shook his head. "No. All that happens tomorrow is evidence of arrest. Always remember, Tim, if you grab the balls the rest comes easily."

Meade cleared his desk, putting his papers in the drawers and the cover on his typewriter.

"They got Raven's picture out on the wire."

Hackett took his feet down. "Those buggers at the ports wouldn't recognize Jesus Christ if he took his beard off. Come on, let's get out of here."

8

RAVEN heard the street door open and shut in spite of the soundproofing. He waited for the key to be inserted in the lock. Soo came in slowly and sat down as if his back hurt. Raven's eyes sought his friend's face. Soo's range of facial expressions was limited according to Western standards. Anxiety was conveyed by a widening of the mouth.

"O.K., what happened?" Raven demanded.

Soo looked him full in the face. "I've just been talking to Berger, the guy in my judo class. Kirstie's in the Chelsea nick. The Drugs Squad busted her at Heathrow this morning."

Bile flooded into Raven's mouth. He found his tongue with difficulty. "What the hell are you talking about?"

Soo's black eyes were compassionate. "It's true, John. I wish to God it wasn't. They found heroin hidden in the back of her camera."

Raven stumbled over the words. "There must be some sort of mistake."

"No mistake," Soo said sadly. "Hackett's working out of Chelsea. That's why they took her there."

"Jesus Christ!" Raven's fingers gripped the chair he was sitting on. "You mean it's not enough to fuck me up. They have to have her as well!"

"Try to take it easy," said Soo. "She's been charged with

possession. She'll be coming up at Horseferry Road in the morning."

All color had drained from Raven's face. He suddenly smashed one fist into his palm, his voice filled with despair.

"What the hell am I going to *do*, Jerry?"

Soo came to his feet. "The first thing you do is get a hold on yourself. I managed to talk to Patrick. He wants you to stay cool."

"Fantastic!" Raven said bitterly. "Kirstie sitting in a cell, 20,000 cops out there looking for me, and what's the advice that I get? Stay cool! Just what sort of a fucking world *is* this, Jerry?"

Soo opened a cupboard and brought a bottle of Scotch. He poured a large shot of neat whisky and gave it to Raven.

"Drink that!" he ordered.

Raven put his head back and swallowed.

"Now listen to me," said Soo. Compassion tinged his voice and manner. "I've told Patrick everything except where you are. He didn't ask, in any case. I told him you were safe. He'll be in court in the morning and he'll try for bail. The best way you can help Kirstie and yourself is by doing what he says. He agrees that it has to be Drake but he needs time to think, to make some kind of plan. Either you trust him or you don't. His words."

Raven heard but his mind was on other things. He shook his head, feeling the Scotch in his veins.

"I just don't understand, Jerry. I may be a whole number of things but at least I'm straight. How *can* this be happening to me?"

"What are you looking for, justice?" Soo said roughly. He poured Raven another drink. "Take this one more slowly. Now listen to me. The name of the game is expediency and Hackett and Drake know the rules."

Raven nodded slowly, a sense of isolation spreading in his brain. He accepted it with a sort of relief.

"I'll tell you what I'm looking for, Jerry. I'm looking for Drake. I'm trying to save two people's lives and I'm that close to the edge." He narrowed his thumb against his forefinger.

Soo's voice was gentle. "I'm here, pal. What do you want me to do?"

The cigarette was suddenly bitter. Raven stubbed it out. "I'm not ungrateful, Jerry. I don't mean to be anyway. It's just that this one belongs to me. I have to do whatever's necessary in my own way. Do you understand that or not?"

"I understand a whole lot more than you give me credit for," Soo replied. "I know how I'd feel if it was Louise in a cell instead of Kirstie. The point is that you *have* got friends who are trying to help you. Don't make it difficult for them."

It was the first time that Raven had seen the other man so clearly concerned and he looked at his friend with fresh eyes.

"There's only so much friends can do," he said. "Can you get hold of some money for me? I'm talking about now, tonight."

Soo looked at his watch. "How much?"

"A thousand pounds. I can get it back to you in a couple of days."

Soo was already on his feet. "I think so, yes. I can try the Cathay Casino. It's run by some people I know. They open at eleven o'clock."

It was five minutes past the hour. "Do you have that much in the bank?" asked Raven. The will in Patrick O'Callaghan's safe bequeathed half his worldly goods to this bandy-legged Chinese. It was something that Raven could never tell him.

"I don't need it," said Soo. "I'm not going to cash a check. We Chinese are men of honor, remember. Added to which, if I don't come up with the money you'll find my head floating past your boat." He zipped up his track suit.

Raven went to the door with him. "This is the last thing I'll ask you to do."

Soo grinned. "I doubt it. I'll be back as soon as I can."

The chapel clock struck the hour. It was oddly quiet for a

city not yet sleeping. Raven waited until he heard the stutter of the Volkswagen and closed the door. It was a quarter to one when Soo returned. He placed an envelope on the table.

"One thousand pounds. I already counted it."

Raven opened the envelope. The money was in twenties and fifties. "Thanks, Jerry."

"My pleasure," said Soo. "Now is it all right for me to go home to bed?"

"Don't jut your jaw," said Raven. They smiled together and their hands met briefly.

"I was going to say something else," said Soo, "but I think I'll save my breath. Just remember the house rules. Out before nine in the morning and not back before six. Otherwise stay in all day and don't breathe. One or the other and you're safe. I'll call you in the morning."

Once alone, Raven picked up the telephone. "Jacek?"

"Not here." The woman's voice was sleepy.

"Can you tell me when he'll be home?"

"Not here," the woman repeated and put the phone down. Raven extinguished all the lights and crawled into the sleeping bag. The face of the clock made a point of light in the darkness. It seemed a long time before he lost consciousness. Cold woke him in the morning. A timing device had turned off the radiators. It was twenty minutes past six. He peeked out through the curtains. It was dark outside but he could make out the roofs beyond the brick wall. The fog had lifted completely. He got the radiators working again and opened the pack of throwaway razors. Then he dressed in Vanders' clothes and made himself tea. The first thing he had to do was buy something else to wear. He switched on the radio. There was still no mention of Kirstie's arrest or of his escape. He took the key that Soo had left on the table. It was seven minutes to eight and Soo had not called. Raven let himself out of the studio. A gray squirrel raced up the trunk of a dead elm and watched Raven cross the sodden grass.

Raven had taken no more than rough bearings the night before when the fog had disguised the buildings and streets. He saw his new surroundings with new eyes. He was between Battersea Bridge and the river. It was a street of modest enterprises rapidly heading for bankruptcy. There was a car junkyard, a tailor's shop with bales of dusty cloth and pictures of long-forgotten actors. A sub-postoffice sold tobacco and candy and there was a Greek fried-fish shop.

He walked with the collar of the mackintosh pulled up, feeling vulnerable. Police would be watching his sister's place and the boat and by now they'd have his picture at the ports. A bus barreled over the bridge traveling southward. Raven boarded it and sat on the top deck, surrounded by the rustle of newspapers in an atmosphere thick with tobacco smoke. He got off the bus in Balham. He knew very little about the neighborhood except that it was a working-class area with a large immigrant population. The day began early here. Some of the stores were already open. People were waiting at the bus stops. Raven bought a couple of newspapers and ate breakfast behind steamed windows in a café across from the Underground Station.

He read the newspapers carefully but there was still no mention of Kirstie's arrest. The omission meant little one way or another. Police news reached the media through the pressroom at New Scotland Yard. Hackett could well have reasons for sitting on the disclosure.

Raven folded the newspapers. It was just after nine o'clock. A Pakistani was taking down the shutters of a store across the street. Raven's idea was to merge with the crowd, to become anonymous yet remain mobile. People rarely noticed the familiar. The plan was gradually taking shape. The Pakistani store was an outlet for camping gear and bike outfits. Raven bought himself a black leather bomber jacket, trousers, and knee-high boots, a spaceman's helmet with visor. He changed into these in a cubicle, dumping his discarded clothing in a plastic bag. His first steps in the heavy boots were clumsy but he was walking normally by the time he reached the builder's skip. He went into a hardware store where he purchased some plastic lettering. He used a public lavatory to stick the letters on the back of his bomber jacket. The legend read:

ARROW MESSENGER SERVICES

His next stop was a half-acre lot a couple of hundred yards away. A few jalopies sat behind barbed wire in front of a wooden hut with curtainless windows. Raven picked his way over duckboards, past a mangy German shepherd snarling on the end of its chain. The man who opened the door of the hut was wearing a muskrat coat that had been made for a woman with the build of a bear. He spoke through the remains of a doughnut.

"Do something for you, mate?"

A board nailed to the door carried the message

BIG BILL'S BIKES FOR BIKIES
BIG BILL GIVES YOU THE BEST FOR COURIER SERVICE

Raven indicated it with his finger. "I crashed. I need a machine. Something that I can use until I get the insurance money."

Big Bill stepped backward, allowing Raven into the hut. There was a kerosene stove, a wooden table with a telephone, two deck chairs, and an electric kettle. A selection of ignition keys hung from hooks fixed in the wall.

The dealer's inspection was shrewd. "What sort of bike are you looking for then?"

Raven could see the choices through the dirty window. A dozen or so machines were propped up on stands under a sloping tin roof.

"I thought you might be able to help," he suggested.

The word brought a frown to Big Bill's forehead. "Help?"

"Advice," Raven enlarged. "I'm working local runs for the moment but I need something reliable."

"Say no more," said the other man. "Come with me."

He led the way across to the lean-to, aiming a kick at the dog as he went. He paused, considering the assemblage of clapped-out machines with the manner of a jeweler displaying a very fine stock of gems.

"How about the Yamaha?" asked Raven. A Yamaha R.D. still carried its plastic windshield.

Big Bill straddled the machine, fishing in his pocket for the right key. The motor caught at the third attempt, filling the shed with the stink of burned oil. He throttled down to a stutter then cut the motor completely.

"Hear that?" His voice was loud in the sudden silence. "Like a sewing machine. Earn a fortune with this little beaut, you will."

Raven's inspection was purely for effect. The odometer reading was thirty thousand miles but the tires were good and the bike was licensed.

"How much?" he asked.

"Five hundred. From you I'll take four seven five."

"I'll buy it," said Raven.

The dealer buttoned the money into a pocket of the flannel shirt he wore underneath the muskrat coat. He wheeled the bike over to the hut, opened a drawer, and produced the registration book.

"You need insurance?"

"I already have it," lied Raven. Insurance involved too many questions.

Twenty minutes later he was riding into Shepherd's Bush, an anonymous figure on a motorcycle, observed but unnoticed. Keglevic's shop was under the railroad tracks, sandwiched between Denton's Discount Fashions and a cut-price food store. The street was one long market, with shops and open-air stands, a neighborhood of bustle and quick turnover. Raven propped the bike outside and pushed open the door. The interior was cluttered with electronic equipment, microchips and transistors, coils of cable. A notice on the wall read

NO RUSSIAN RADIOS REPAIRED

A large man appeared in the inner doorway. He was as tall as Raven and built like a buffalo with a mane of coarse gray hair. He wiped his hands on his overalls, looking uncertainly at Raven.

Raven lifted the visor. "Hi!"

His first involvement with Poles had been as a Detective-Inspector breathing down the neck of Casimir Zaleski, a memorable rogue whom Raven had come to like and respect. Zaleski was dead. Keglevic was his cousin. The Pole threw his arms wide, revealing a bank of gold-backed teeth.

"So!" he roared. "Is ex-Inspector-Detective Raven!"

He hugged Raven hard and drew him into the inner room. The workbench there was littered with bits of cannibalized computers. Gobbets of solder gleamed on the dirty plank floor. A stained aluminum coffeepot was bubbling on a gas jet. An icon representing the Black Virgin of Cracow hung on a wall. Beneath it was a forty-year-old photograph of Keglevic wearing the uniform of a pilot-officer in the R.A.F. A Distinguished Flying Cross was pinned to his chest.

The Pole washed a couple of mugs, filled them with coffee, and added coarse brown sugar. He pushed a chair at Raven and sat on the other. His slate-colored eyes took in Raven's attire.

"So," he said comfortably.

"I need your help," said Raven. He could have told the Pole the truth but there was no need to burden a friend with more than was necessary.

Keglevic nodded. "So what can I do for you, mate?"

"I need a device."

Keglevic obviously approved of the word. "What kind of device?"

Raven explained. Keglevic listened, moving his shaggy head from time to time.

"You telephone my house last night?" he asked suddenly.

"Yes," said Raven. "Give your wife my apologies."

Keglevic's wave made light of the matter. "Not necessary. Hanka is awake in any case. She is waiting for me to come home. Your brother-in-law who is teaching London School of Economics. Bastard!" He spat at the floor.

"Yes," said Raven. His sister's husband, a Pole of a younger generation, had recently announced his allegiance to Trotskyism.

"His father and grandfather good soldiers. Bloody bastard!" Keglevic made a pistol of his thumb and forefinger and fired it at his temple.

Raven's shoulders lifted. "I feel the same way but there's nothing we can do about it."

"No good," said Keglevic. "How soon you want this device?"

"How soon could you make it?" asked Raven. It was unlikely that Kirstie's case would come on before eleven-thirty. Magistrates' courts heard the lesser offenses first, the drunk and assault cases.

Keglevic refilled his mug from the pot. The coffee had the clout of a jackhammer and Raven declined.

"Is not difficult, the making," said Keglevic. "Is only difficult finding proper parts. I have to look. How far you want this thing to work?"

"As far as possible," answered Raven.

The Pone glanced up. He was sketching on a pad with a felt-tipped pen. "Quarter mile?"

Raven nodded. His friendship with Keglevic went back to the days of Zaleski's Wielka Polska Restaurant. Keglevic's modest store concealed the fact that he was one of the best electronic engineers in the city with twenty years' training in a Decca experimental station.

The Pole was still drawing his circuits. He glanced up. "Not much noise. Just tick-tock like clock. Loud then soft depending how far signal is traveling."

"Would anyone else be able to hear it?" asked Raven. "I'm talking about someone with a phone in his car."

"No." Keglevic balled the piece of paper and aimed it at the can that served as a trash basket. He reached inside his dirty overalls and produced a gold half-hunter watch. "Is different frequency. I have it ready as soon as possible. Phone me."

Raven felt the weight of Keglevic's arm around his shoulders. The Pole had made no reference to the way that Raven was dressed nor would he seek to know the reason. Like many Poles of similar background Keglevic had reached freedom by way of Italy and remembered his sojourn there with nostalgic affection.

"Ciao!" he said.

9

DRAKE checked his watch. It was almost seven o'clock. He had slept better on his second night of freedom, waking refreshed. He opened the curtains and looked outside, scratching through his hair. The fog had completely vanished, leaving a damp mild day. He was determined to be at the magistrates' court as soon as it opened. He wanted to find a good seat, somewhere where Raven would see him. He wanted the proceedings to be a carbon copy of what had happened all those years ago, only this time it would be Raven who would be standing in the dock.

Drake stretched and padded downstairs with bare feet. The newspaper he had ordered was lying on the mat in the hallway.

He took it into the kitchen and made tea and toast. There was nothing in the paper about a raid on a houseboat. He had waited until four o'clock on the previous day before calling Hackett. He'd tried six times during the next three hours but without success. He put his plate and cup in the sink and went upstairs again. He picked up his passport and sat on the side of the bed, studying the new Brazilian visa. He was determined to see Raven sentenced but once that was over the house in Brazil was waiting. He had owned it for more than nine years, a pink-washed presbytery set among dusty coconut palms. The village was reached by paddle steamer from Bahia, a day-long trip through water infested by crocodiles. There had been two good reasons for his choice of Vale de Yeguas, its remote position and an endless supply of teenage girls willing to act as housekeepers. It was a refuge taken care of by the couple who worked and lived off the land, a place to soak up the sun for a few months before moving on. He no longer thought much about the future. For the last six years his mind had only carried him forward as far as Raven's destruction. Everything stopped at that point. The prospect of what he would do with the rest of his life was in a sense an anticlimax.

He lifted the phone and dialed Hackett's home number. "It's me," he said.

There was a pause before Hackett answered. His voice was strained. "I don't know how to say this, George, but we lost him."

Drake's ears roared. "What the fuck are you talking about, lost him?"

Hackett appeared to be speaking from a distance. "There was nothing we could do. He went over the side of the boat in the fog as we were taking him off. But we got the girl."

A sudden pain gripped Drake's chest. He wrenched at the collar of his pajama top, gasping for air. The pain passed but he felt exhausted.

Hackett's tone sharpened. "Are you there, George?"

"I'm here," Drake said grimly.

"Look, I'm sorry," said Hackett. "But there was no way we could have prevented it, nothing we could do. You couldn't see ten yards and the dogs were useless. By the time the River Police arrived the bastard had vanished."

It was crystal clear to Drake that six years' resolve and planning, the perfect plan for revenge, had just been destroyed by this clown. He brought his mouth very close to the phone, his voice bitter and menacing.

"You'd better listen to me, you prick! You've got forty-eight hours to find him. If Raven isn't in a cell by this time the day after tomorrow that tape's going to be on the Commissioner's desk."

He put the phone down with a shaking hand and sat for a while trying to marshal his thoughts. Instinct told him that he had lost. Raven had been a cop himself and knew all the moves. Not only that, he had friends and money. He might well be out of the country by now, sitting somewhere safely while his friends turned the Establishment upside down in his defense. And if they ever got to Hackett, Hackett would be looking to protect himself. Still, there was no evidence that Drake had been part of the frame. No one had seen him on the boat. The heroin had come from Hackett. With Raven at large, Hackett was expendable.

Drake started dressing slowly, feeling as though he had not slept at all. The girl would go free if he dumped on Hackett but he had never had any real interest in her. He used the phone again, calling Varig Brazilian Airlines. There were three flights a week from Heathrow to Rio de Janeiro. Wednesday, Friday, and Sunday. He booked a seat for the following day, arranging to pick up the ticket later.

He was calmer now that he had made his decision. There was enough money left in the safe-deposit box to pay his immediate expenses. Once in Rio, he could draw on his Swiss account. He still had one visit to make but there was no rush for that. He could mail the package from Heathrow. He'd be in Brazil before it arrived at the Yard. He found a piece of brown paper and wrote the address in capitals.

**THE COMMISSIONER OF POLICE
NEW SCOTLAND YARD
S.W. 1**

(PERSONAL AND CONFIDENTIAL)

The shape and size of the package would ensure kid-glove treatment, probably by the Bomb Squad. And once opened, the contents would prove as explosive as nitroglycerine.

He spent the day leisurely, not bothering to go near the court. He collected his ticket, ate crabs in Wheeler's, and took in a movie. The *Evening Standard* carried an account of the proceedings at Horseferry Road.

CANADIAN PHOTOGRAPHER CHARGED WITH DRUG OFFENSES

Kirstie Macfarlane, thirty-two, a Canadian photographer giving an address in Paris appeared in front of Mr. Gurney, Magistrate, charged with being in possession of one third of an ounce of heroin. Detective-Sergeant Berger of the Drugs Squad gave evidence that Miss Macfarlane was stopped at Heathrow as she was about to board an Air France plane for Paris. She was searched and the heroin was found in the back of a camera that was in her luggage. She was taken to Chelsea Police Station and charged. Detective-Chief-Superintendent Hackett told the court that further and more serious charges would follow. The accused lived as common-law wife with a man called John Raven who was wanted in connection with the same offenses. The police had the strongest objections to bail and asked for a remand in custody. Mr. Patrick O'Callaghan for the defense said that Miss Macfarlane was prepared to surrender her passport, offer substantial sureties, and reside at an address that the police could designate. Denying bail, Mr. Gurney remanded Miss Macfarlane in custody for eight days.

It was dark when Drake returned to the mews. He parked in front of the house, walked around to the alleyway, and entered through the garden. He put the grocery bag with the cold meats and salad in the kitchen, poured himself a drink, and switched on the television. He'd give people time to settle down before driving out to Forest Hill.

10

HACKETT was sitting on one of the benches outside the courtroom. The vestibule had emptied. All the Drugs Squad officers had gone except Meade. Hackett's aide was talking to Patrick O'Callaghan, a slim elegant figure with an Elizabethan beard and wearing a rosebud in the lapel of his pinstriped jacket. One glance at him had been enough for Hackett. He had the feeling that the defense lawyer was about as harmless as a cobra and wanted no dialogue with him. What Hackett needed was time to think and in order to think he needed solitude. There was small prospect of this at the moment.

Drake's reaction was more or less what Hackett had expected. The truth was that Raven had vanished, gone to earth like an old fox wily in the ways of survival. There was no question about it, Drake blamed Hackett and would happily sink him without trace. Meade crossed the vestibule. His conversation with the defense lawyer had ended. O'Callaghan was getting in the elevator.

"He wants her suitcase," said Meade. "He says there are things in it that she'll need in Holloway."

"Give it to him," said Hackett. Meade was projecting the tough street-cop image with his slouch hat and trenchcoat.

The younger man glanced across at the clock. "What do you have in mind, Guv?"

"Go on back to Chelsea," said Hackett. "I've got things to do. I'll talk to you later."

Back in his car, he opened the glove compartment. Inside was a thirty-eight automatic fitted with a silencer, an assassin's weapon taken from a Hong Kong hit-man. There were 4,000 officers in the Met trained in the use of firearms. Not only was Hackett one of them, he held a marksman's proficiency certificate with both pistol and rifle. He returned the gun to the glove compartment, turned the key, and drove to Gerrard Street. It was time to pay his dues.

This was Chinatown and he walked slowly, savoring the strong spicy smells, the bite of salt fish, the occasional reek of opium rising from a grated cellar. Only the old men used it now, smoking the stuff in basements or rolling pills that they chased with minute cups of hot sugarless tea. Hackett glanced neither left nor right but he was fully aware of what was going on around him. People who saw him either froze or faded into doorways. His presence on the street would be known long before he reached his destination. He turned right at the Dragon Social Club and climbed two flights of stairs to a mahogany door bearing a polished brass plate. The legend was engraved in both English and Chinese.

THE MANDARIN TRADING COMPANY
(Registered in the Crown Colony of Hong Kong)

A television camera angled in the ceiling surveyed the landing. Hackett pressed the bell and spoke into the entryphone. Thirty seconds passed, then the door was opened by a Chinese with cropped gray hair wearing a dark-gray tunic. He took Hackett's coat, indicating the red and gold couch in the hallway. In more than a dozen visits Hackett had neither heard him speak nor seen him smile. The servant ushered Hackett through a doorway.

Art had no meaning for the Superintendent but he recognized luxury and the splendor of this room always impressed him. There was jade in profusion, green and smoky-white fashioned into horses, serpents, and dragons. The walls were draped with silk tapestries, the teak furniture lacquered in red and gold. Priceless Ming porcelain stood in alcoves. The servant closed the door without sound.

"Please sit down!" Lam Po Hong was a short man in his sixties with an American accent and wearing a well-tailored business suit. He opened a cigar humidor and pushed it across the desk. He neither smoked nor drank but his hospitality was unbounded.

Hackett shook his head. He had received Hong's summons shortly after Drake had called. He found the timing ominous. A picture frame on the desk partially obscured Hong's view. He removed it, his voice courteous.

"Inquiries are being made about a man called Lee Fook."

Hackett smiled cautiously. There were at least six more rooms in the suite of offices but no sound ever seemed to come from them. It was the same every time that Hackett came here. The only people he saw were Hong and the servant. Yet he knew that behind those closed doors bodyguards were waiting. Hong had survived numerous attempts to assassinate him and never moved a yard on the street without an armed escort. In Chinatown Hong *was* the law, The Wise One.

"Who's making the inquiries?" asked Hackett.

Hong's delicate nose became even thinner. "Customs and Excise officers. You know I don't like these people. I don't want them in the area. They bring trouble."

Hackett considered his nails. This would be the opening gambit. Hong never adopted a frontal position. Hackett looked up.

"Do *you* want Lee Fook?"

The Chinaman placed his fingers together. His smile was wintry. "I would as soon have cancer, my friend. I do not want him, I need to know where he is."

"He's locked up in a room over a pub in Bermondsey," said Hackett. "He's a witness in a case I'm handling. I'm keeping him there for safety."

"This case," said Hong. "Is it connected with the arrest of the Canadian woman?"

Hackett looked at him, shark-eyed with alarm. This bastard knew everything.

"As a matter of fact, yes," he admitted.

"And what happened to the man Raven? Why wasn't he in court?"

"He escaped," Hackett said flatly.

Lam Po Hong shook his bullet head. "I am disappointed in you, Mr. Hackett. We have a long association based on mutual trust and benefit. If one of these elements is missing the association is placed in jeopardy."

Hackett blinked. "I'm not too sure that I understand what you're getting at."

Hong's mouth smiled but not his eyes. "You have a position of authority with a thousand eyes and ears. When something happens that could affect my interests I expect to be told. When a woman is arrested at Heathrow airport carrying heroin, I expect to be told about it in detail. Your duty is to me first, remember, Mr. Hackett. Who *is* this woman?"

"She's a Canadian photographer living with an ex-policeman called Raven. He's the man who escaped." Hackett didn't like the way that the conversation was going.

Hong was making notes on an ivory-backed pad. "What is the total amount of the heroin involved?"

"An ounce and a quarter."

Hong's eyebrows drew together. "Has it been analyzed?"

"Not yet," said Hackett. He was getting in deeper with every statement. He tried for the ring of sincerity. "I intended calling you at home this evening. I was waiting to get as much information together as I could."

Hong leaned forward. "I want this man Raven caught, Mr. Hackett. This is essential. I dislike competition from people I have never even heard of. Do I make myself clear?"

Hackett nodded. "He's not going far. The seaports and airports are blocked. It's a matter of time before we get him."

Hong took a turn to the window and back. "Have you seen our old friend since he came out of prison?"

A danger signal flared in Hackett's brain. The one thing that Hong must not know was that his name figured on the tape.

Hackett made a sign of denial. "No, I haven't. He called me the day after he was released and suggested a meeting but quite frankly it didn't seem to make sense. I can't afford to be seen with George Drake. Has he been in touch with you?"

"No," said Hong. "But I can tell you where he was last night. He was in the Lotus Room on Fulham Road, eating alone. He's not dangerous, is he?"

"*Dangerous?*" Hackett tried to make the suggestion sound laughable. "Hell, no. I mean, so many years have gone by. It's too late for all that. But don't get me wrong. George and I are still friends. He understands why we can't see one another. In any case he's off to Brazil."

Hong's smile was brilliant. "That is good news. I don't trust him. Goodbye, Mr. Hackett. I shall expect to have news of this Raven."

On the way downstairs Hackett was surprised to find his shirt sticking to his back. He bought a bundle of kebab sticks in a Soho grocery store and walked back to his car. As he drove away, a space-helmeted motorcyclist pulled out twenty yards behind.

●

Hackett spent the afternoon at New Scotland Yard, studying the papers Berger had brought back from the Director of Public Prosecutions' office. It was dark by the time he reached Fulham Road. He slipped a pair of handcuffs in his pocket together with the thirty-eight. Then he pulled on a pair of gloves. He left the car two blocks from Savernake Mews and walked to the alleyway behind Drake's house. He peeped through the back door keyhole. The lights were on in one of the downstairs rooms. He walked around to the front of the house. Drake's car was parked in the mews. Hackett placed his finger on the bell. He could hear the noise of a television set. He waited for thirty seconds but nothing happened. He was on the point of ringing again when Drake's voice sounded from the other side of the door.

"Who is it?"

Hackett kept silent. He heard the spring lock being manipulated. The door opened an inch. Hackett wasted no time. The full weight of his shoulder landed against the door. Drake staggered back, grabbing at the wall. Hackett kicked the front door shut and stuck the gun against Drake's neck.

"*Move!*"

He shoved Drake into the sitting room and sat him down on the sofa. "Get your clothes off!" ordered Hackett.

Drake started removing his jacket. He let it fall to the ground and took off his trousers. His face was stony. Hackett used a foot to hook the clothing toward him.

"Face down on the floor, your hands behind your back!"

Drake obeyed, stretching out awkwardly. Fat sagged above the top of his jockey shorts and there was a hole in the heel of his right sock.

"Hands behind your back!" Hackett repeated.

Drake's arms came up slowly. Hackett slipped the cuffs over Drake's wrists.

"Spit your teeth out!"

Drake was lying with one side of his face pressed against the carpet. His jaw and tongue worked uselessly. Hackett bent down, pressing the end of the silencer into the back of Drake's neck.

"Bite me and I'll blow your brains out!" He used his left thumb and forefinger to remove Drake's dentures and lodged them in an ashtray. At least the bastard wouldn't choke on them. He started to go through Drake's pockets. The haul was interesting. There was between five and six hundred pounds in cash, a Varig flight ticket to Rio dated for the following evening, and a couple of keys on a ring. One of them was finely tooled and bore a number and the letters E.S.D. *Exbury Safe-Deposit!* Hackett knew the bank well. It was only a quarter mile away from Scotland Yard. He picked up Drake's jacket. An inside pocket held a New Zealand passport and driving license in the name James Muldoon. Both documents carried Drake's picture. Two Brazilian visas were stamped in the passport. One was six years out of date, the other was valid.

Hackett turned his attention to the desk. In the second drawer he opened he found a folded sheet of brown paper. He read the printed address and looked down at Drake.

"The Commissioner of Police?" said Hackett. "You dirty bastard!"

Drake rolled his eyeballs. His face had collapsed with the removal of his teeth and his voice had altered.

"You've got it all wrong, Henry. I wasn't going to send it."

But Hackett was searching the room, dumping the contents of drawers on the floor, stripping bookcases. There was no sign of the tape. There was nothing up in the bedrooms except Drake's clothes. The house keys were lying on a table in the hallway. Hackett returned to the sitting room. Drake was still in the same position. Hackett sat on the edge of the sofa, making his point by jabbing Drake in the side with the end of the silencer.

"Let's get this thing in proper perspective. You've been biding your time for years to pull the plug on me. You always intended to do it. *Right?*" snarled Hackett.

Drake had become an old man with piteous eyes in a sunken face. He made no reply.

The idea of Drake's betrayal outraged Hackett. "There you are," he said. "Sitting on a fucking plane on your way to Brazil leaving me up to my ears in shit. Ruined. Career gone and staring at four walls. And if that isn't enough, Hong's hatchet men waiting on the off chance that I manage to beat your little number. There was no way I could win, was there, George?"

Drake mumbled something but the words made no sense. "How many tapes did you make?" Hackett demanded. A tic had inserted itself into his left cheek.

Drake's lips moved. "One. There was only one."

"Bullshit," said Hackett. "If you'd said ten or twenty the answer would still have been bullshit. I wouldn't believe you if the Pope was holding your hand."

Drake managed to raise his body, shaking with the effort. "I tell you there is only one."

Hackett's eyes locked onto Drake's face. "O.K., where is it?"

Drake's head collapsed on the carpet. "It's no good telling you where. I'd have to take you there. We can still work this thing out, Henry. I've got money."

Hackett came to his feet. "Money? I'm going to take every goddam thing that you own before I'm finished with you. But first I'm going to learn the truth. There's nothing like pain for concentrating the mind."

He picked a book from the floor and rapped the hard cover with his knuckle. Then he pulled the bundle of kebab sticks from his coat pocket. He broke one in half. Each half was about three inches long. A strong sense of indignation made his voice almost righteous.

"See this?" he demanded, pushing the sharpened stick under Drake's nose. "I'm going to shove it up under one of your fingernails. I've got a strong feeling that you'll tell me the truth about the tapes. Anyway, let's see how many nails have to go before I believe you."

Drake's face had lost all vestige of color. His eyes were dull and frightened. Hackett knelt down and lifted Drake's cuffed wrists. He selected a finger and inserted the sliver of wood under the nail. Then using the flat of the book as a hammer, he drove the stick down with one sharp blow. Drake screamed like a maimed rabbit, his body jerking as though charged with a thousand volts. His feet and head rose from the floor, stiffened, then both hit the floor at the same time.

The violence of Drake's reaction startled Hackett to his feet. The book dropped from his hand as he stared down at the body on the floor. Hackett had seen death too many times. Drake's eyes were open but they were sightless. Hackett fumbled desperately for the key and removed the handcuffs from Drake's wrists. Dark blood oozed from the wounded finger onto the carpet. The embedded kebab stick made a livid line extending as far as the second knuckle. There was no vestige of a pulse.

Hackett's mind thrashed as he looked at the dead man, uncertainty edging toward fear. He turned his head sharply, sensing that someone was standing watching him from the hallway but there was nothing there except the grandfather clock.

Hackett stepped over Drake's body. The dead man's face had turned gray. Pictures flashed without sound on the television screen. He had to get out of there as fast as he could. There was no time to put things in order. He left the contents of Drake's pockets where they were, taking no more than the keys on the ring. He opened the French doors and stepped out into the garden. The curtains swung back into place. The spring lock clicked shut. It was impossible to see the body on the floor through the chinks in the curtains. He climbed the wall at the end of the garden and dropped down into the alleyway. There was no noise anywhere. He dusted himself off, removed his gloves, and walked back to the parked Cortina. It was difficult to control his voice when he picked up the phone.

"Tim? It's me. Look, I'm stuck twenty miles out of town. No, its just another of those false leads. Someone was supposed to have seen him in Chertsey. Is there any news your end?"

"Not a thing, Guv," said Meade.

"Then I'll talk to you later," said Hackett. He locked the gun in the glove compartment. His nerve was returning. It could be days before Drake's body was discovered. Evidence of torture would ensure that the death would be treated as murder. Hackett's only regret was that Drake had died without revealing where the tape was hidden. He was unable to make up his mind whether it would be one tape or several but on balance he settled for one. Drake had never trusted anyone else in his life.

Hackett remembered the keys in his pocket and held them in the palm of his hand. Suddenly he knew the truth. There would be one tape and he knew just where he would find it.

11

RAVEN was some thirty yards behind when the Cortina pulled to the curb. He cut his motor and propped the machine on the stand, screened by the line of parked cars. This was a quiet thoroughfare with Victorian houses fronted by gardens and running parallel with Old Brompton Road. Deep shadows lay beyond the circles of light shed by the street lights. Suddenly Hackett's head came into view above the car roofs. Raven whipped off his helmet and boots, stuffed them in the pannier and donned the nylon mac and sneakers. His feet made no sound as he went after Hackett. Raven could see through the archway into the mews. The stretch of cobblestones was deserted except for two parked cars. Footsteps clicked behind him. He stepped sideways into someone's garden. He crouched down, peering through the bushes. A couple went by, chatting about a party they were about to attend. Hackett was standing behind a car in front of the last house on the right in the mews. He bent down quickly as headlights came on. When the car had passed Hackett stood up again. Raven could see him clearly, ringing the doorbell. More footsteps forced Raven to duck again. By the time the street was clear, Hackett had disappeared.

Raven walked into the mews, his hand on the butt of the revolver in his pocket. A light was burning in the transom of the house where Hackett had been standing. Raven lifted the mailbox flap and peeped through into the hallway.

A Burberry coat and a hat were hanging on a stand next to a grandfather clock. The black homburg with its greasy binding bore the unmistakable stamp of George Drake.

Raven turned sharply, sensing movement behind him. There were no lights in the house opposite but he had a strong feeling that he was being watched. He went through the motions of ringing the doorbell, shook his head as though disappointed, and walked round into the alleyway. The feeling of being watched stayed with him. There was a door in the garden wall. Looking through the keyhole, Raven could see the lighted windows. A shape passed behind the curtains. Then the French doors opened and Hackett emerged. Raven ran for the far end of the alley. The Superintendent hurried off in the opposite direction. By the time Raven reached the street, the Cortina was approaching Old Brompton Road.

Raven wheeled his machine into the alleyway and propped it against the back door. The revolver was in his pocket. He had no idea what was happening between Drake and Hackett but his own luck seemed to be changing. He had waited outside Horseferry Road magistrates' court, an anonymous figure on a motorcycle. Patrick O'Callaghan had arrived in a cab, passing Raven without as much as a sideways glance. People came and went, police, witnesses, defendants surrendering to their bail. Squad cars and Black Marias turned into the yard. No one paid any attention to the courier in the space helmet.

There was a glimpse of Detective-Chief-Superintendent Hackett, crossing the street flanked by members of his squad. They walked with easy assurance, joking as they went. There was no sign of Kirstie. In a way Raven was glad. Seeing her would only have increased his agony.

It was after one o'clock when Hackett came down the steps from the court building and made his way to a red Cortina. It was then that Raven straddled his bike and started the motor. He had never been far from Hackett since.

He stood up on the saddle and hauled himself over the wall. The curtained windows were only fifteen yards away. He crept forward, the gun in his right hand. The French doors were firmly closed. A chink in the curtains offered a glimpse of the room beyond. All he could see was a television set and the back of a sofa. There was no sound coming from the television but pictures flashed on the screen. Raven felt his way along the wall, past a window that was too small to crawl through, as far as the kitchen. He heard a tap dripping into the sink under the window. He stepped back, retaining an outline of the room in his brain. Table, sink, dresser, refrigerator.

He had to move fast, preserve the edge of surprise. There was no time for finesse. He followed his shoulder through the broken window frame, showering glass into the sink as he clambered down. Five steps took him into the hallway. In spite of the noise he had made, the basic pattern of sound in the house remained constant. The grandfather clock ticked on. He jerked the white door open, moving in a crouch, holding the gun. His impetus carried him forward and he stumbled over the bare legs in front of him. He steadied himself, staring down at the half-naked body. Drake was lying face-down on the carpet, his head twisted sideways. Worms of blood oozed from his nostrils. His face had completely collapsed. Raven saw why. Drake's dentures were sitting in an ashtray.

Raven backed off, wiping the palms of his hands on his trousers. The floor was littered with books and papers. The room had been ransacked, drawers left half-open. Drake's jacket, boots, and trousers were on the sofa. On the desk was a large sum of money and a New Zealand passport and driving license. Both were in the name of George Drake. The Varig Brazilian Airlines ticket to Rio was dated for the following night. Drake's right hand was bent in an unusual position. Raven lifted it. A splinter of wood had been driven down under one of the fingernails as far as the knuckle.

Raven's stomach suddenly betrayed him. He ran for the kitchen, trying to control his heaving as he leaned over the sink. He found a whisky bottle and drank from it, remembering the marks on the dead man's wrists. Drake had been handcuffed and tortured. It was difficult to understand why Hackett would have gone to such lengths.

Raven climbed the stairs. The one bedroom in use had also been ransacked. Had Hackett found whatever it was he had been looking for, there would have been no need for torture. It had to be something that he needed desperately. Something perhaps that gave Drake this hold on him, the reason that forced him to be part of Drake's scheme.

It was hardly the way that Drake would have wanted things, yet in a sense his death clinched his vengeance. It left Kirstie in a cell and Raven on the run, a fugitive doomed to ultimate capture. Unless – and the possibility was growing in Raven's mind – unless Hackett could be put in Drake's place and forced to reveal their joint secret.

Raven made his way down the stairs. He was almost at the bottom when he heard the noise of tires on the cobblestones. He moved quickly to the window. A car was ghosting into the mews. A couple of men leaped out. One of them rang the doorbell of the house opposite. Raven raced through the sitting room and wrenched open the French doors. He was halfway down the garden path when he heard men's voices in the alleyway. He pulled himself up and stood, teetering as he sought his balance. He had a brief glimpse of startled faces below and then he was gone, running along the top of the wall. Despair planted his footsteps surely as pursuit pounded behind him. A car was driven to the mouth of the alley. Headlights came on. Raven's shadow leaped ahead of him, past yelping dogs and lighted windows.

He dropped at the end of the alleyway. A fresh burst of speed gained a few yards. He couldn't go on for much longer. The movements of his legs were becoming leaden and labored. He was running on a street that was a copy of the one at the far end of the mews. Lights shone in the windows and over the gardens. A small car stopped abruptly in front of him. The woman driver was already crossing the pavement, house keys in hand as Raven drew abreast. He pushed after her into the hallway, no thought on his mind but refuge. He closed the door and stood in the darkness, holding the revolver to her head. He could feel her whole body shaking.

The noise of running feet invaded the street outside as his pursuers burst out of the alleyway. Raven heard a car being driven slowly toward him. Then the chase ended. A man shouted, careless of being heard.

"He's doubled back, Mick! Get in the car and we'll cut him off!"

Raven pushed the woman forward under the light of a lamp hanging from the ceiling at the bottom of the staircase. She was older than he had thought, in her middle thirties with lank brown hair and a pale, frightened face. She was clutching her purse to her breast and wearing some sort of woollen garment that hung below the hem of her raincoat. Raven herded her into a kitchen with flowered wallpaper. A half-eaten bowl of cat food stood on a mat inside the back door. Raven took a swift look through the curtains. The light shafted across unkempt flowerbeds to a blank brick wall.

He whirled as a woman's voice sounded in a speaker on the dresser. "Alice?"

He laid his finger against his lips and tiptoed out into the hallway. A cat emerged from a room at the top of the stairs, arching its back, tail lashing. It sidled down into the kitchen. Raven followed and shut the door. A switch nullified the intercom box on the dresser.

"Who is it?" he demanded.

She looked at him fearfully. "My mother. She's a cripple."

"Speak to her," he said. "Tell her everything's all right."

She switched on the system again and bent to speak. Her body was still shaking.

"It's all right, Mother!" she said.

The other woman's voice was querulous. "But I heard a man talking! Who have you got down there?"

"It's Mr. Robins, Ma. Mr. Robins from the Library. We're going through the plans for the new speed catalogue."

The mother's voice grumbled on. "Really! I don't see why you have to bring your work back here, Alice. I call it most inconsiderate of them."

Alice's eyelids fluttered. "I'm sorry, Ma. I'll be up in a minute." She dropped the switch again, looking at the gun in Raven's hand. "Please don't hurt me. I'll do whatever you want. There's almost a hundred pounds in the next room. Take it!"

He put the gun in his pocket, wanting to reassure her. "Look, I don't want your money. I don't want to harm you. Believe me. All I want is your help. Do you live here alone?"

She nodded, her pale-lashed eyes still afraid. "There's only the two of us, in the flat I mean. There are people upstairs and in the basement but we live alone."

"The people upstairs, do they use the same entrance?"

She moved her head from side to side. "They have their own."

He leaned his back against the door. "Do you know who those men were just now?"

"Yes." Her voice was almost inaudible. "The police."

It was suddenly very important that she should understand.

"That's right, the police," he said. "They were after me. And I'll tell you why they were after me, Alice. Somebody framed me, planted heroin on my boat. And they did the same thing to my girlfriend. She's in jail and I'm on the run. Do you understand now why I'm here?"

Her fingers found her throat uncertainly. "But that's terrible! I mean you don't look . . ."

"Like a criminal? Look, a *policeman* planted that dope! The head of the Drugs Squad. It may sound incredible but it's true, Alice."

The statement left her unsure. "I don't know," she said. "I mean I don't know what to think. I'm frightened."

"I'm frightened, too," he said quietly. "But we don't have to be frightened of one another."

They stood in silence, watching the cat toy with its food. "I'll have to go upstairs," she said, turning to him." She'll be suspicious if I don't. I'll tell her that you're staying for a snack."

Years of nose blowing had left broken veins on both sides of her nostrils. He found room to pity her.

"Is there a phone upstairs?" he asked gently.

She nodded. "Yes, but I give you my word of honor that it won't be used. I won't betray you, I promise."

He opened the door for her, gauging the distance to the street door as she climbed the stairs. She was back almost immediately, having found time to brush her hair and put on some perfume. She left the kitchen door ajar. Her manner now was almost conspiratorial.

"She can't hear what we're saying but she'll know if the door is closed. I'm afraid there isn't much to eat but I can scramble some eggs."

"Eggs would be good," he said. It was almost eight o'clock. The police search might have been called off but he still had to get out of the neighborhood.

She scrambled the eggs, made toast, and some very bad coffee. She ate nothing herself, content to watch Raven. A couple of times she looked as if she were about to say some-

90

thing. Either she changed her mind or lost courage. She collected his plate and stood there waiting for his instructions. Her submissiveness made him feel guilty.

"I'm going to have to borrow your car," he said. "Do you have a spare set of keys?"

The police would have his new description and it would be routine procedure for cars to patrol the area.

"Please!" she said. "I only have the one set of keys and I really do need my car for work. I'll drive you wherever you want."

Her hopelessness increased his feeling of pity. "O.K., then we'd better go."

She put on her coat and called from the foot of the stairs. "I'm just going to run Mr. Robins home, Ma. I won't be long!"

The grumble from upstairs followed them to the door. Raven glanced right and left then beckoned her outside. He sat beside her in the passenger seat, his long legs uncomfortable in the cramped space. She donned a pair of spectacles and switched on the lights and motor.

"You'll have to tell me where it is that you want me to go."

He rolled down the window. "Drive past the mews, slowly."

He looked down the length of the alleyway. His motorcycle was no longer there. "Well, at least they're thorough," he said.

She turned her head sideways, her expression puzzled. "I'm sorry?"

"The police," he replied. "It doesn't matter. Do you know how to get to Sloane Square?"

For some peculiar reason the question put a touch of starch in her manner.

"I've lived in London all my life."

"Well, that's where we're going," he said.

They drove in silence, Raven's mind in a cell with Kirstie. The car stopped at the bottom of Sloane Street. Alice kept the motor running. He stood on the pavement, looking through the open window.

"Goodbye and I'm sorry," he said. There seemed little else that he could say.

She managed a tremulous smile. "I hope you were telling me the truth. But good luck, anyway!"

He waited until the taillights of the Mini had disappeared before joining the line at the bus stop. There was safety in numbers. A number nineteen bus turned the corner. He climbed to the top deck and sat near the stairs. It was twenty-five minutes to ten by the clock outside Chelsea Town Hall. He glanced right as they crossed Battersea Bridge. The *Albatross* was in total darkness but he knew that men would be somewhere nearby, waiting.

His sense of loneliness was increasing. He needed someone to talk to, someone who would listen to the truth and understand. He left the bus and turned right at the Cypriot fish-and-chips shop. It was Drag Night in the pub and cars had been left up on the pavement. Raven threaded his way through them. Once beyond the wall it was very quiet. The only light was the glow that hangs over London at night. He let himself into the studio and stretched out on top of the sleeping bag, the revolver on the floor next to him. The chapel clock struck the quarter hour, the sound depressing him as it had since the days of his childhood. The phone rang. It was Soo, speaking as though he was firing the words through his teeth.

"Just where the hell have you been?" he demanded. "I've been calling for almost an hour!"

"I've been out," said Raven.

Soo seemed enraged by the word. "Look, John, are you completely out of your mind? The whole building's been buzzing since just after seven. They found your bike and they found Drake's body. The woman living opposite Drake called the police. Just what is going on?"

"Hang on a minute!" Raven found the bottle of Scotch. A quick slug made a pool of warmth in his stomach.

Soo's voice was agitated. "They're saying that you killed Drake, for God's sake. What the hell is going on?"

Raven spoke very clearly. "I killed no one, Jerry. I'd been tailing Hackett all day, ever since he left court this morning. I followed him to Drake's place. I saw him go in and I saw him leave. Drake was already dead when I got into the house."

"Jesus Christ!" said Soo. "Look, there's only one thing left to do, John. I'll get hold of Patrick and you'll have to turn yourself in. We'll go to Patrick's friend in the Home Office."

"I'm turning myself in to nobody," Raven said flatly. "I'm going after Hackett."

Soo spaced the words. "You are definitely crazy. In the first place how can you be certain that Hackett killed Drake?"

"That's a stupid question, Jerry," said Raven. "I tell you I saw him go in and leave. He left the same way that I did, over the back wall. That house had been ransacked. Hackett was definitely looking for something. Do you know that Drake had a piece of wood driven up under one of his fingernails? Did they tell you that?" He poured himself another Scotch.

"Are you drinking?" Soo demanded.

"I'm drinking," said Raven. "I'm going after Hackett, Jerry. He's the man with the answers."

Soo's voice was sardonic. "You're in great shape to go after Hackett. With 20,000 cops looking for you. It's murder now, John."

But the word didn't touch him. "I haven't killed anyone," Raven repeated. "And just as long as I stay free there's a chance of proving it. I've got no chance from a cell. Look, Jerry, it's the same old argument. There *is* only one way for me to go!"

Soo's voice was resigned. "I give up. If you're determined to commit suicide then there's nothing I can do about it."

"I have no alternative," argued Raven. "Don't you see that, Jerry?"

"Don't ask me what I see," answered Soo. "I'd rather not tell you. Just don't go near Hackett's home. He'll be expecting it."

"I won't go near his home," said Raven. "I don't even know

where he lives. But I'm going to keep on top of him. It's my only chance. He'll realize that he was followed and he'll change his car. Is there any way of knowing if he goes to the Pool?"

Soo's answer was grudging. "It's possible, I suppose. Yes."

"If he does, how soon could you let me know?"

"He could borrow a car anywhere," Soo objected.

"I said if he goes to the Pool. How soon can you let me know?" It had almost become an act of faith.

"Tomorrow morning." Soo gave Raven a number. "Call me there at ten-thirty sharp. It's a café near Victoria Station. Now try to get some sleep. There's an outside chance that you might wake with more sense."

"It isn't sense that I need," said Raven. "It's luck."

He brushed his teeth, undressed, and crawled into the sleeping bag. He lay in the darkness, shutting out all thoughts of failure. He knew what he had to do, no matter how tough it might turn out to be.

12

IT WAS ALMOST half-past nine when Hackett made his way into the building. Half the lights were out but officers were still dealing with reports of killings, rapes, and robberies. As the old-timers said, a cop worked until the time came to stop. There was only one entrance to New Scotland Yard and the benches in the central hall were crowded with the usual collection of dazed and troubled complainants. There were tourists with tales of having been fleeced by three-card tricksters, embarrassed men telling how hustlers had given them keys that didn't fit doors, bewildered women who had been jostled and mugged by teenage gangs at bus stops. Uniformed officers sitting at the counters dealt with each woeful tale patiently, steering the victim into the interview rooms to be further questioned by the detective branch.

Hackett made his way toward the elevators, his warrant card already in his hand. Security officers checked the credentials of everyone who entered the building. There were no exceptions, no matter how familiar the face or how often the occasion. He heard his name called and turned around. It was Dusty Rhodes, a Scotland Yard character, a bachelor on permanent night duty at his own request. Rhodes had a nose like a hound and the reputation of knowing everyone who worked in the building. He worked out of Criminal Intelligence, the unit that handled police undercover work, collating rumors and tip-offs. Once C11 marked a suspect for total surveillance he was nearing the end of the road.

"The old man wants you," said Rhodes, winking.

Hackett's stomach turned over but he managed to get a grip on himself. Higher echelons often used Rhodes as a confidential runner. Hackett sent the elevator skyward. The door at the end of the corridor bore the sign

ENTRY TO AUTHORIZED PERSONNEL ONLY

Commander Bolt was standing at the uncurtained window with a backdrop of distant towers behind him. He was a tall stooped man with a spare face, thin gray hair, and alert eyes. An untidy tweed suit and a pipe gave him the look of a schoolmaster. He took the pipe from his mouth.

"Sit down, D.C.S.," he said, waving a hand. "You're an elusive bugger!"

After the first quick glance, Hackett avoided looking at the top of Bolt's desk. A cop was watched by a disembodied eye from the moment of his first salute. The eye might blink occasionally but never for long. Few in the ranks managed to time the blink correctly. Up until now, Hackett had always managed it.

Commander Bolt remained standing, tamping down the tobacco in the bowl of his pipe.

"Something the matter with your car phone?" he asked, over the flare of the match.

Hackett knew how to look earnest. It was a matter of raising the chin and firming the mouth. "No, sir. I was off the air. Out of London, meeting a contact."

Bolt used a second match to ignite the tobacco. All the furniture in the building was supplied by the Department of the Environment. Grade for grade in terms of seniority, it was the same as in most government offices. Bolt's personality was expressed by silver-plated cups that recorded his athletic prowess since he had first joined the army. One was inscribed *Cadet W. F. Bolt Victor Ludorum Pirbright 1946.* Another commemorated his last triumph as *Staff-Sergeant W. F. Bolt Military Police Three Mile Champion Aldershop 1953.*

Bolt's appointment was new and gave him roving authority within the Serious Crimes Squads. He was known to be in favor with the Commissioner. It was the third time the two men had met; Hackett both feared and disliked him.

Bolt's eyes were fixed and unwinking, like a bird's. He puffed smoke from the side of his mouth.

"Have you heard the news about Drake?"

"Drake?" Hackett repeated guardedly.

"Come on now, Superintendent! Your old boss!"

Bolt's jovial manner could have been guile. His manner provided no clue. Hackett affected a sudden understanding.

"Well, I saw his name on the Discharged Prisoners List if that's what you mean, sir."

"Then quite obviously you *haven't* heard," said Bolt, talking as he dealt with his pipe. "He's dead. Murdered."

Hackett tried to speak but no words came. It was incredible that they had discovered the body so soon.

Bolt's manner held a mild kind of enthusiasm. "They found him in a mews house in Fulham with something rather nasty stuck under one of his fingernails. The preliminary medical report indicates that death was due to a massive coronary."

"Good God!" said Hackett. His mind was hurdling one obstacle after another.

"Yes," said Bolt. "How did you feel about him?"

Hackett approached the question cautiously. He was fairly certain that no one had seen him with Drake but he had to be careful.

"*Feel*, sir? I'm not quite sure what you're asking me."

Bolt's smile had no warmth at all, a mere widening of the mouth. "You were close to him. You worked together for years. What happened must have come as a great shock to you surely? I'm referring to his conviction."

Hackett cleared his throat. "Of course I was shocked, sir. I mean, it was something like learning that your father's a thief. But I'd like to get one thing very clear. If it hadn't been for George Drake I'd still be in Wapping, wearing out shoe leather. Most of what I know as a cop I learned from him."

Bolt's face showed understanding. "I appreciate your feelings, Superintendent. But the man was a rotten apple, a villain who deserved everything that he got. However, that's not the point. He served his sentence. And everyone has the right to live."

Hackett shook his head. "I'm sorry if I'm not making much sense, sir. I don't really know what to say."

The corner of Bolt's mouth was making small popping noises as he sucked on the pipe stem.

"Ordinarily Drake's death wouldn't be any of your business but it seems that we have a lively suspect. It's your man, Raven."

Hackett's stomach was barely under control. "*Raven*, sir?" The surprise was genuine.

"That's right," said Bolt, scratching the small of his back

against an open file. "Apparently a woman called Belper lives in the mews opposite Drake. It seems that she saw someone acting suspiciously and called the police. Western Robbery took the job but they arrived on the scene a few seconds too late. Raven went over the back wall. But a couple of officers did get a sighting and there's no doubt about identification. They found the motorcycle that Raven was using."

Hackett searched his memory, looking for a motorcycle in his rearview mirror. It was the moment to bluff hard.

"May I ask a favor, sir?"

Bolt drew his eyebrows together. "You know, my toes always curl when I hear that remark."

"I'd like to take over this investigation," said Hackett. Even to his own ears it sounded just right. There was the proper blend of interest and dedication.

The response surprised him. "That's precisely what I had in mind," said Bolt. "There are some very interesting angles here. There's Raven's involvement with Drake and your own inquiries. In fact the drugs scene in general. I've been talking to the Director of Public Prosecutions' office. They seem to think that Drake's death could well be treated as murder. After all, we've got a criminal act resulting in a fatality."

"Yes, sir," said Hackett. The scenario could not have been better had he written it himself.

Bolt spoke looking out through the window. "You've got to catch this fellow, Chief Superintendent. The Commissioner's asked for a full report on the case. There's one aspect though that I'll confess I'm not too happy about. I'm talking about this phone tap on Detective-Inspector Soo's home."

"With respect, sir, it was necessary. He and Raven were at Police College together and the association goes back many years. And we know they've been on holiday together since Raven left the Force."

Bolt turned. "Very well. We'll come to something else. I had a call this afternoon from Customs and Excise, someone by the name of Edmonds. Know him?"

"No, sir," said Hackett.

"He says you've been poaching."

Hackett blinked. "Poaching, sir?"

"This informant you're using in the Raven case. Lee Fook, is it?"

"Yes, sir. What about him?"

"Customs want him for questioning in another matter," said Bolt. "But they say they can't find him. Edmonds claims that you've buried him somewhere."

Buried was hardly the word. Lee Fook was locked in an upstairs room over Danny Schwartz's pub as naked as a newt and getting a daily ration of dope. When the time came, they would throw him his clothes and he would be word-perfect.

"What I'm asking you," said Bolt, "is whether this man is essential to your inquiries."

It was time for the frank open look, the appeal to esprit-de-corps. "He's vital, sir. He's been buying from Raven for almost two years. And to be perfectly honest there are very good reasons for keeping Fook away from Customs and Excise at the moment. I'd rather not have to go into details."

Bolt squinted over his pipe. "Say no more, Superintendent. Western Robbery knows that you're taking over. Ask for Detective-Inspector Harlip. I understand that Drake's body has been taken to the mortuary. Is there anything else that you want to know?"

Hackett came to his feet. "I don't think so, no, sir."

"Then keep me informed," said Bolt. "The Commissioner's breathing down my neck on this one. We've got a couple of snipers in the House of Commons. We don't want to give them fresh ammunition. The word is *action!*"

*

Hackett drove north to Finchley. Western Robbery worked out of what had once been a section house for bachelor officers. The Robbery Squad was a completely independent unit that utilized the facilities of the adjoining police station. The Squad consisted of sixteen plainclothesmen driving unmarked cars, specialists relying more on tip-offs and narks than pure detection. The duty officer's name was Solothurn, a man of thirty wearing beads, sweatshirt, and a Mexican mustache. He made it clear that as far as he was concerned, someone else was entirely welcome to the Drake assignment.

"Once you're into drugs," he said, "you're on a hiding to nothing."

Hackett glanced around the untidy office. "Where are Drake's things, Detective-Sergeant?"

Solothurn handed him an envelope with the contents of the dead man's pockets. Hackett inspected them for the second time and supplied a signature.

"That's everything?"

Solothurn nodded at the bag on the chair. "There are some clothes there. That's the lot."

"What about the scene-of-crime report?" Hackett picked up the magazine that Solothurn had been reading.

The Detective-Sergeant both looked and sounded bored. "The prints have gone to Forensic. The body's at Horseferry Road Mortuary."

Hackett dropped the magazine and took Drake's bag. "Happy enough with things out here, are you, Sergeant?"

Solothurn grinned. "That's one thing you can bet your ass on. We've got a good bunch and we stick together."

Hackett's mask dropped, revealing his snarl. "I'm glad to hear it. If you want to keep it that way, learn to show respect to superior officers."

He drove back to Savernake Mews, still upset by the incident. Drake's front door was badly splintered. He used Drake's house keys to open the one surviving lock. It was strange to be back in the darkened hallway. His fingers found the light switch. All the doors in the house were wide open. He turned on more lights. A square of hardboard covered a broken window in the kitchen. That would be Raven. The implication that he had been tailed disturbed Hackett deeply.

A chalked outline on the sitting room carpet marked the position where Drake's body had lain. Everything else had been left exactly as it was, books on the floor, drawers half-open. Hackett's mouth firmed as he saw Drake's dentures in the ashtray. Perfect, he thought. People who missed a full set of false teeth might well have missed the safe-deposit key. He considered the right place to claim that he had found it and decided on a drawer up in Drake's bedroom. That was it, at the back of a drawer, under the paper lining.

He turned out all the lights, locked up the house, and crossed the mews. Drake's Ford was still parked outside the front door. Hackett pressed his thumb on the bell. A dog started yapping.

The woman's voice was suspicious. "Who is it?"

"Police," said Hackett.

The door opened slightly and a woman's face appeared. "But I've already talked to the police!"

"This is different. Detective-Chief-Superintendent Hackett." He moved forward, holding up his warrant card.

She led him into the hallway, a small woman with coils of white hair wearing unbecoming stretch pants. She was carrying a pink-eyed poodle in her arms. He followed her into an over-decorated room where a single log was burning in the fireplace. A cup of chocolate stood on the hob in front of it.

"I was just about to go to bed," she said.

He smiled reassurance. "This won't take long. You *are* Mrs. Belper?"

"Yes," she said, then dropped the poodle and clapped her hands. The animal fled upstairs. She sat down on the sofa next to Hackett. He showed her Raven's photograph.

"Have you ever seen this man before, Mrs. Belper?"

She nodded vigorously. "Of course I have. That's the man I saw in the mews!"

He put the photograph back in his pocket. "You're quite sure about that?"

She drew her mouth into a rosebud. "You don't know me,

Superintendent. I'm not the sort of woman who makes that kind of mistake. *Really!*"

Time was passing and he was getting edgy. There was a lot to do. "Look," he said. "I'm a busy man with a long night ahead. I want you to tell me exactly what you saw this evening. And try to keep it brief."

Her displeasure was clear. "I'm not too sure that I like your manner, Mr. Hackett. You're hectoring me."

He made a quick change of mood. "I'm sorry. Let's start again."

She took the cup of chocolate from the hob. "Well, I got back from the country shortly after five o'clock. Driving tires me these days, you know, so I went upstairs to rest. I suppose I must have dozed off. Do you know I've *no* idea what made me go to the window, Superintendent!"

He realized that he was being asked for a comment. "Curiosity?" he hazarded.

She shook her head. "A premonition, more likely. Anyway, when I did look out there was this man standing in front of Lucy Mellor's house. There was something very strange about the way he was acting. Something *suspicious*." She paused. "Don't you take notes, Superintendent?"

"Keep it all in my head," he said. "So you called the police, right?"

"No," she said. "The dog was barking so I went downstairs. By the time I came back the man had disappeared. Well, believe it or not, a few minutes later *another* man appeared and started doing the very same thing! *That's* when I called the police!"

Hackett's voice faltered for no more than a second. "How long an interval was there between seeing these two men, Mrs. Belper? Five minutes, ten—longer?"

"Oh, dear," she said, putting the empty cup down. "Now you're making me nervous. Well, it was certainly longer than ten minutes. I'd say about a quarter of an hour. That's it, a quarter of an hour."

"And you got a good look at them both?"

She shook her head. "Not really, no. The second one, yes. You see I wasn't paying too much attention to begin with although I must say there have been some very strange goings on in the house since that poor girl went to France. Of course I blame the agents entirely. They seem to show no discretion at all. I mean that woman who was there, the one with the drunken husband. And now this person, going in one door and out the other. If you ask me he was highly suspicious himself!"

"How about the first man you saw?" His manner was casual. "Do you think you could give a description of him?"

Her expression was doubtful. "Well, he had his back to me. He wasn't wearing a hat. That's one thing I'm sure about."

"How about height?" he asked. "Was he taller than me, shorter?"

She looked him up and down. "Definitely taller. And rather well dressed. Do you think he was a confederate?"

He breathed easier. Danger had receded. "I doubt it. It was probably just a coincidence." He came to his feet and gave her a card with a telephone number. "You've been of great assistance, Mrs. Belper. If anything else occurs to you, please get in touch."

She looked at the card with interest. "Does this mean that I'll have to give evidence, Superintendent? I've never been in a court, you know."

He shook his head, smiling. "Don't worry, Mrs. Belper. We'll take good care of you."

He buried the Cortina in a long-term parking building, taking the gun with him. He used a pay phone in the entrance.

"This is Detective-Chief-Superintendent Hackett. I need a Pool car for tomorrow."

The man's voice was unenthusiastic. "This place is looking like a breaker's yard at the moment. I've got seven vehicles crashed in thirty-six hours. It doesn't say much for the standard of driving."

"Look, officer," said Hackett. "What I want is a car, not a state of the nation speech."

"Hang on," said the voice. "I'll see what I can do." He was back on the line in a couple of minutes. "I can let you have a Rover V8, Superintendent, but it won't be ready before six o'clock. Will that do you?"

"Six o'clock," said Hackett. "I'll be there."

He walked the half mile to the apartment building, going through a couple of supermarkets on the way. A man on a motorcycle might fool him once but no one on two legs could tail him and not be noticed. He climbed the two flights of stairs, let himself in and watched the ten o'clock news. But his mind was on other things. He made himself a salami sandwich and poured a drink. The ash grew long on his cheroot before he had his plan perfected. All he needed now was the nerve to carry it through.

He woke up early. The window was three feet from his bed. What he saw outside he had seen before thousands of times, the low flat roofs that were wet in winter and dusty in summer with pigeons wheeling and strutting. He owned two rooms, kitchen, and bath in the worst part of North Kensington. The elevators no longer worked and the walls were daubed with graffiti. The light fixtures in the hallways and passages had been ripped out. White faces were rare now in the neighborhood. But Hackett had lived there for eighteen years and saw no reason to move. His affair with Mildred Drake had taught him a lesson. No lady since then had shared his life for longer than a weekend. He had had a few heads broken, organized a few arrests, projected an image of wrath and authority that the local bloods respected. Pensioners might be mugged in other parts of the neighborhood but never on Bulstrode Street. Hackett's contact with what was left of his family was minimal and friendship something that he had never needed. Power was the only thing in life that he craved and at fifty years of age he'd achieved it. Now its very source was endangered.

Drake's death had changed nothing. The threat of the tape still remained. He filled the kettle with water and sat at the table watching it boil as he always did. His sleep had been broken by a dream of Drake shuffling like a beggar, eyeballs rolling. The dream incorporated Hackett's deep anxiety. But he told himself that if he kept his head he could still survive. Events had started to turn in his favor. He resented the outrageous thing that Drake had done to him and failed to understand his own stupidity. Knowing Drake the way he did, it was fatal to expect anything but to be sunk without trace. Had he only had sense enough to realize this all those years ago, he could have protected himself in so many ways.

He was sure now in his heart that the tape would be found in Drake's safe-deposit box. He drank his tea and nibbled a piece of toast, assessing his strengths and weaknesses. Raven was the only other person who knew the truth about Drake's death. And because Raven was smart he would have worked out Hackett's motive for being involved in the frame-up. No one had as much as lit a cigarette for Drake in the name of friendship during the whole of his life. Raven must reason that Hackett's motive would stem from fear.

Hackett shaved and put on one of his formal suits, 300 pounds' worth of blue hopsack tailored by a man who owed Hackett a favor. Black shoes and a dark tie completed the image of a senior detective, alert of mind and of sober behavior. He was at the Yard by quarter to nine. Meade had beaten him and was in the big office, his fingers covered with the usual carbon smudges. His image was changed; he was wearing checked trousers and a turtleneck sweater today.

"Morning, Guv," he said breezily. "I'm not quite sure how he managed it but O'Callaghan got into Holloway after visiting hours last night. He took Macfarlane's bag in."

Hackett drew Meade outside into the corridor. "Have you heard the news?" Meade shook his head. "Drake's dead. Raven killed him last night."

Meade's mouth fell open. "Jesus Christ, Guv! What are you saying? No, I heard nothing!"

"They found the body in a mews house in Fulham," said Hackett. "The people up top are worried about this one, Tim. We've got the case."

Meade's eyes were lively. "Surely Raven's overreached himself this time, Guv'nor! But how the hell does Drake get in the act?"

"It's a long story," said Hackett. "Hang about, Tim. I've got to go upstairs and see Bolt. I'm going to need you later."

Meade wagged an invisible tail. "I'll be here."

Commander Bolt was in his office, drinking coffee from a plastic cup. Hackett threw him a token salute.

"Good morning, sir. You told me to keep you informed. I went to Savernake Mews last night, did a bit of snooping. Incidentally, I talked to the witness, Mrs. Belper. She's reliable enough, I'd say. She makes no bones about it. Raven's definitely the man she saw."

Bolt put his cup on the desk. "It's amazing. Everybody sees him except us! Where *is* the bugger hiding?"

"We'll get him," Hackett said confidently. The night before it had been Bolt who stood and Hackett who sat. Now the positions were reversed.

Bolt brooded for a moment. "We've got a man in possession of drugs, evidence that he's been selling on a fairly large scale for some time and we've got a bent ex-copper who's dead. Now what's the link, Chief Superintendent? Why did Raven kill Drake?"

Hackett had spent time framing the answer to this sort of question. He offered it with conviction.

"I've been doing some homework, sir. What we do know is that Drake maintained contact with the drug scene even in prison. There's a report from the authorities that he associated with a convicted dealer inside, a Chinese. My own theory is that Drake discovered something about Raven's own involvement with the drug scene."

Bolt raised his head, his eyes widening. "You mean black-mail?"

The kite was airborne. Hackett took it a little higher. "Drake came out of prison three days ago. There's been plenty of time for him to have contacted Raven and shown his hand."

"Wait a minute!" Bolt used his empty pipe as a pointer. "Who put you on to Raven in the first place?"

Hackett shook his head regretfully. "I'm sorry, sir. I can't reveal the source of my information." He was safe enough there. The subject was confidential and he had the protection of the law.

"Can't or won't, D.C.S.?"

"With respect, sir, won't." Hackett took the Kleenex containing Drake's dentures and placed them on the desk. He put the safe-deposit key beside them. "I found these in Drake's house. The key was hidden in a drawer. The teeth were in an ashtray. Western Robbery missed them both."

"Put those bloody things away," Bolt said hastily, looking at the dentures. He turned the key over in his fingers. "E.S.D.?"

"Exbury Safe Deposit, sir. It's a quarter mile away. I'd like a search warrant."

Bolt nodded and pushed the key back across the desk. "I'm getting flak and that's something that I don't like." There was an implication that whatever Bolt incurred in the way of censure would be passed on.

Hackett took the key. "I've got a feeling that this can give us the lead we want, sir."

Bolt leaned back in his chair. "Have you seen the medical report on Drake? Lacerations on the wrists, a splinter under his fingernail. This was torture, Hackett."

It was time to apply the brakes, gently but firmly. "I've talked to people who served on the Force with Raven," said Hackett. "O.K., so he was a troublemaker, someone who set himself above the law, but people who knew him find it difficult to think of him as a killer."

Bolt's manner was unimpressed. "They'd probably find it

difficult to think of him as a dealer in hard drugs, come to that. No, the man's into something that's run away with him."

Hackett pretended to give it some thought. "Drake had a false New Zealand passport and driving license. He was supposed to be leaving the country today."

Bolt's smile was tight. "If he'd known what was coming he'd have been out of there quicker than a bear with a bee up its ass! How about the girl, do you think she knows where Raven might be?"

"No," said Hackett. "I've got a feeling that she doesn't know too much about anything. In fact I think that Raven was using her. I think he planted that dope in her camera."

Commander Bolt's face displayed a look of distaste. "The more I hear about this bugger the less I like him. He sounds like a thoroughly unpleasant piece of work." He leaned forward to make his point. "Watch your step with Detective-Inspector Soo. They think a lot of him upstairs and there could be hell to pay if you're found to be out of line."

"I won't be found out of line," said Hackett. His confidence was growing by the minute. "There is one other thing, sir. It would make our job a whole lot easier if Raven's picture is released to the media. I think the time has come."

Bolt scribbled on a pad. "Picture and search warrant. I'll have a word with the A.C.'s office. I don't suppose they'll refuse but as far as the picture's concerned you'd better leave the details to them."

"Thank you, sir." Hackett permitted himself a token smile. "We'll get him. I give you my word on it."

*

The downstairs office was crowded. Hackett had a word with one of the men who was keeping an eye on Lee Fook.

"How are things over there, Jamie?"

Detective-Constable Parrish believed whatever his superiors told him. If he queried anything about the method of Lee

Fook's detention there was no suggestion of it in his manner.

"He's complaining about the cold, Guv. He keeps telling us how warm it is in Hong Kong. We got him another heater."

"Keep him happy," said Hackett and caught Meade's eye. He nodded his aide into the inner office.

Meade closed the door and stood there expectantly. Hackett's look was meaningful.

"Nothing that's said here must go any further, Tim. Is that understood?"

The terrier strained, alert to do its master's bidding. "You know me, Guv!"

"Yes, but there are others in this building who talk," Hackett said significantly.

Meade cocked his head. "Are you talking about anyone in particular?"

"I'm talking about canteen chatter," said Hackett. "Saloon bar gossip. Who's doing what and why. We're getting closer to Raven, Tim, and there's a man out there with his ear flapping. Detective-Inspector Soo. We're sunk if he knows what we're up to."

Meade shifted his wad of gum. "I got the impression that you didn't think that Soo would be in contact with Raven."

Hackett shook his head. "Then you got the wrong impression. What I said was that we wouldn't *catch* him in contact with Raven. But I'd bet a month's pay that he is. No, you could put a round-the-clock tail on that slant-eyed bastard and he'd still manage to give you the slip. I found this key in Drake's bedroom, Tim. Raven and Western Robbery missed it." He held up the key so that Meade could see it.

Meade's face assumed a knowing look. "You think that's what Raven was looking for?"

"I'm certain of it," Hackett replied. "This key's going to solve our problems, Tim. That's why security's so important. Nobody knows about it except Bolt, you, and me. I'm getting a search warrant to open the box. Meanwhile I want you to go to Savernake Mews, take a good look at the place in day-light. Maybe there's something else that we missed." He gave Meade Drake's house keys.

"Will do," Meade said smartly. "What about the Murder Squad? Aren't we sort of treading on their toes here?"

Hackett stretched his arms wide. "We'll let our betters worry about that. In any case it'll probably wind up as manslaughter. Remember, Tim, this is between you and me. I'm relying on your discretion."

Meade braced himself as if a medal had just been pinned on his chest. "I'll take Berger with me. He's no mastermind but he keeps his mouth shut."

"Good thinking," said Hackett. "There's one other thing, a witness in the mews, a Mrs. Belper living in the house opposite Drake's. Keep well away from her. She's nervous."

It was twenty minutes before a messenger arrived with the search warrant. This authorized Hackett to "open and search a safe-deposit box held in the name of Drake or Muldoon in premises at 208 Exbury Street, S.W.1, and to seize the contents therein."

The telephone rang. It was the Assistant-Commissioner's office. Raven's picture would be issued to the media during the course of the morning. Hackett locked his desk and left the building. Exbury Street was no more than a short walk away. He stopped at a record store and bought a cassette. He intended to switch the tapes. It would be up to someone else to decide why Drake would have kept a recording of Beethoven's Fifth in a safe-deposit box.

Production of the search warrant galvanized the guard on duty at the bank entrance. Hackett was shown straight into the manager's office. The official received him with clear distaste. Hackett lost no time in dealing with him.

"You do your job," said Hackett. "And I'll do mine. And let's try to make things as pleasant as possible."

The manager returned the search warrant and unlocked a file. He talked as he looked through the contents.

"I don't like this sort of thing, officer. We're a highly respectable organization and we take the utmost precautions. I mean we have to. Mr. Muldoon's references were impeccable."

"I'm glad you think so," said Hackett. "It so happens that Mr. Muldoon was a convicted criminal called Drake."

The manager came around the desk, his face stiff with indignation. "I intend to accompany you. It's regulation procedure in a case like this."

"Please yourself," said Hackett. "Just as long as you understand that this is a legal search. Any attempt to obstruct it would be contempt of court."

They went downstairs to the vaults. A guard behind a grille released the gate. The manager's tone was brittle.

"This gentleman is a police officer."

The guard timed the visit and handed over a second key to the manager. It complemented the one in Hackett's hand. A second gate led to a corridor and four large vaults. Each vault was lined with steel boxes sunk deep in concrete. The manager used his key, indicated the second lock, and withdrew to an alcove. Hackett turned the key and pulled the drawer. Inside was a sheaf of thousand-dollar bills and nothing else.

He turned to see the manager watching him. "I shall need a receipt for that money," said the man.

The receipt was typed in the manager's office. Hackett signed it and left the bank with a deep sense of foreboding. He was too shaken to face anyone until he had pulled himself together. He located a bench and sat down, the pigeons foraging at his feet. He had been certain that the tape would be found at the bank. He thought back, trying to put himself in Drake's place but without success. The fact remained that the tape existed. It contained the substance of every crooked deal that Hackett had made with his old chief. Dates, places, sums of money, the actual voices and conversations. It was out there somewhere, where it could be found by accident, played out of sheer curiosity.

His right hand strayed in his pocket, touching a flat piece of metal. He found himself looking at the Yale key that had been on Drake's ring. It was a key like millions of others, dulled by age and usage. *Yet Drake had been carrying it!* Hackett hurried back to the Yard and surrendered Drake's dollars to the Custodian's Office. Then he locked himself in his room and used the phone.

"This is Detective-Chief-Superintendent Hackett. I'd like to speak to the prison governor." He explained what he wanted.

"I'll have to call you back," said the official. "Is Drake in some sort of trouble again?"

"In a manner of speaking, yes," said Hackett. "He's dead."

The Governor was on the line in a couple of minutes. "I have his Visit and Correspondence file in front of me. The only mail he received was from a firm of solicitors in Victoria. They visited him here on two occasions in connection with his divorce. As for your last inquiry, I'll read from his Property Sheet. He entered prison with twenty-eight pounds and thirty pence cash, various papers, a yellow metal Omega watch, a black plastic comb, and one Yale latchkey."

"Thank you, Governor." Hackett put the phone down, his pulse beating marginally faster. He knew now that the key had been in Drake's possession at the time of his arrest. It had to be important or Drake wouldn't have hung on to it. The trick now was to find the lock that it fitted.

He leafed through the telephone book but he could find no listing for Mildred Drake. An operator informed him that the number was unlisted. Hackett took his request to the supervisor and used his authority. He dialed and a woman's voice answered.

"It's me," he said quietly. "Henry. I have to see you, Mildred."

"Good God!" She sounded as though she had just seen death.

"I'll be there at seven," he said and hung up.

The years zigzagged back to the first time he had met her. He remembered the Masonic Rooms hung with paper chains, the colored balloons lifting in the hot air as eighty sweating cops pushed their partners around the dance floor to the music of Mick Flaum and his Sharps and Flats. Hackett had gone with a W.P.C. from the Vice Squad. George and Mildred Drake had been among the company. Hackett recalled thinking at the time that she seemed a cut above Drake's beer-and-sausage image. She was a tall woman with copper hair and a tight ass, uneven teeth and a fine skin that was just beginning to web. He had danced with her twice and she left with his phone number. A month later she spent the night at his flat. The affair was to last eighteen hectic months, a year longer than he wanted. Her demands increased as time went on, the scenes becoming more dramatic and tearful. There were impassioned pleas for Hackett to take her away, threats of suicide, that she was asking Drake for a divorce. Hackett had reached his decision overnight, putting her bag outside the door and calling a cab for her at seven o'clock one Sunday morning. It was six months before he finally managed to get rid of her, refusing to answer her letters, accepting none of her phone calls.

At a quarter to six he took a cab to the Metropolitan Police Motor Vehicle Pool and found the place buzzing with news of an intruder. A man had appeared with a fake delivery of spare parts. Challenged, he had made off into the night. Opinions differed as to his intentions. Once Hackett had the man's description from the security guard on the gate, he knew who it was. His fear of Raven was growing. He had the Rover up on a hoist and checked the undercarriage carefully. The mechanic watched him sardonically, a dead cigarette between his lips.

"What you looking for, Super, bombs?" he asked.

Hackett held out his hand. "Just give me the keys!"

He headed south, constantly checking the rearview mirror, running the Rover in and out of service stations and once through a car-wash. By the time he reached Forest Hill, he was sure that he had not been followed. The address he wanted was halfway up a steep rise. He drove on past the house and stopped near the crest of the hill. There was an impression of space up here. A hundred thousand points of lights twinkled in the darkness stretching to Hampstead Heath. He stood for a while, listening to the sounds carried by the wind. His ear detected nothing more sinister than the growl of a gear-change as a car climbed below.

He started walking down the hill. Bare trees lined the pavements between the street lights. There was enough light to see the outlines of the houses and gardens, the whimsical arrangements of fancy-trimmed hedges and garden gnomes. He lifted the latch, made his way down the path and rang the doorbell.

13

MILDRED DRAKE's hand was shaking as she put the phone down. Hackett's voice persisted in her mind. *I have to see you, Mildred.* It was eleven years since he had thrown her out of his life, producing a sudden and misplaced loyalty to her husband as an excuse to end their affair brutally and irrevocably. But the truth had been apparent for months, in his eyes and in his touch. She had served her purpose and was expendable. Yet his voice still had the power to set her stomach churning.

She moved in front of the oblong mirror, staring at her reflection with angry eyes. She was fifty-four years old. Age and drink had blurred the outline of her face, coarsening its fineness, marring the skin with broken veins. She smiled carefully, exposing Mr. Warwick's patient work. She had confined herself to the house for two months, moving only as far as the surgery, while Warwick pinned, crowned, and replaced her teeth.

Hackett's betrayal had completely destroyed her morale. By that time, Drake had moved out of the house. She sought a new personality, giving up smoking, attending yoga classes and meditating. She meditated for the best part of a year then the truth was revealed to her. The two men she had loved in her life had both proved to be shits so the hell with men! She would never again be vulnerable. Meditation and yoga were forgotten. She started smoking once more and discovered the solace of Scotch.

She lifted her shoulder-length hair with a coquettish gesture. Drinking and the care of her hair were her two main extravagances. The inspection continued. Her breasts were flat under the stained housecoat but her legs were still good. She lit a cigarette and sat down. It was cold in the room but she could no longer afford to keep the central heating on all the time. She was vaguely aware that the house was dirty, the furniture unpolished and dusty. She tended to forget and she dropped things.

She poured herself a large Scotch and water and glanced at the clock. The condition of the house didn't matter but her own appearance certainly did. She smiled again languorously, eased by the alcohol seeping into her bloodstream. She must look her best for Prince Charming. She carried her glass up to the bathroom and lay in hot soothing water, the whisky glass on the edge of the bath clouding in the steam. She dried herself, slowly powdered her body, and wrapped herself in her robe. Then she sank the rest of her Scotch. She closed the curtains in her bedroom and opened the clothes closet. A row of plastic hangers was suspended from the rail. It took some time and the assistance of another drink before she was able to make up her mind what to wear. A clean bra, panties, and seamed stockings to start with. Then a slip to wear under the clinging black wool dress. The Jean Muir model was nine years old but it still looked good. The thought made her giggle. If Aunt Barbara had known the use to which her money had been put she'd revolve in her grave. Clothes, new teeth, and liquor. She giggled again. *Henry, my love, it's all for you!*

It was almost five o'clock. She put on every piece of jewelry that she owned, her aunt's heavy gold bracelets rattling down her thin forearms. She shielded the fine wool dress with a hand towel and applied Max Factor makeup to her face. A touch of Collyre Bleu to the eyes, Nina Ricci behind the ears and on the wrists then she stepped back from her reflection, her head cocked on one side. Not bad, she thought. Not bad at all. She pirouetted and turned the bedroom lights out.

The peanuts in the kitchen were stale. She reroasted them under the grill and banged ice cubes out of the container. Her whisky was blended. There was no malt for Henry but he should have his ice. He would see that she remembered. She carried the peanuts and ice into the sitting room and switched on the electric heater. It took some time to find Hackett's two records in the pile of dusty albums. Sinatra's voice came from the recesses of the room, singing of the days of wine and roses. She turned down the volume, winking at herself in the oblong mirror. She was feeling good now, no tremors, no anxiety. Nothing more than excitement at the prospect of seeing a man who had been her lover. Her only real lover.

The phone rang at six-fifteen. It was Hackett. "Just checking," he said. "Are you alone?"

"I'm alone," she said, her pulse beating a little faster. But she felt herself poised and urbane.

"I'll be there in ten," he said and hung up.

She heard the car stop higher on the hill and followed his footsteps along the pathway. When the chimes rang she rose and opened the front door. He hadn't changed much. A few lines here and there, a little puffy around the eyes. His hair was longer but it still shone like a crow's wing. He was wearing a blue cashmere overcoat with tan Italian loafers. He stood for a while, looking at her, and then opened his arms. She wanted to move her mouth as he bent to kiss her but his lips brushed hers.

"Come in," she said. "Let me take your coat."

He followed her into the sitting room, smiling as he heard the Sinatra record playing. She poured his Scotch and addded ice.

"Cheers," he said, lifting his glass. "It's been a long time. Too long, in fact."

She felt strangely elated as if something tremendously exciting was about to happen.

"You heard about George?" he asked after a while.

She nodded. "They phoned from the Yard this morning. Nobody seemed to know that we'd been divorced."

"Routine," he said. "Somebody looked up the next of kin. Has anyone been to see you? I mean any other officers?"

She moved her head from side to side. "No."

His voice had a ring of sincerity. "I've always felt bad about us, Mildred. I mean the way that we left it. I suppose the truth is that we never had a chance."

She crossed her legs and lit a cigarette. "I realized that a long time ago. I've no regrets."

"*I* have," he answered, his eyes searching hers. "Whenever I think about what might have been."

She couldn't bring herself to look at him, disturbed by the intensity in his voice.

"Anyway," she said. "You're here and that's what matters."

His eyes flickered. "It must have been a shock for you to hear that George had been killed."

She shook her head, auburn hair bouncing on her shoulders. "How can you say that, Henry! You know very well that George and I hated one another for years. He loathed me before I met you and he loathed me afterward." She showed him the brilliance of her new smile for the first time. "What happened to all that old charm, Henry? You haven't even told me how I look."

He wet his lips with the tip of his tongue. "You don't need me to tell you that you look good."

"Oh, but I do," she said. "It isn't every day that an ex-lover pays a call. My *only* real lover, come to thnk of it! I didn't know what to think when you called but I made an extra special effort." She tilted her head and fluttered her false eyelashes.

His face narrowed, his fingers finding his fleshy nose. "Are you drinking a lot these days?" he demanded.

She remembered the pose all too well and was able to spray its fire. She rose and wiggled her way to the drinks cupboard. She poured herself a half-tumbler full of Scotch and topped it with water. Then she sat down again, smiling.

"Henry," she said, "I drink when the mood takes me. Loneliness is a terrible thing."

He put his glass down, his voice sugary. "There's no need for a woman like you to be lonely."

Her eyes opened wide. "What are you trying to say to me, Henry?"

He shrugged, his change of direction pointed. "George was murdered, Mildred. I'm in charge of the investigation."

She found the news highly amusing. Her bracelets rattled as she sipped her drink.

"That's certainly one for the book. Together in life and death. You, George, and me. It's a pity he's not here to appreciate your interest."

Hackett shook his head in a rebuke. "I don't like to hear you talking this way, Mildred. It isn't you."

"Oh, but it is," she said. There were things about her that he would have to relearn. "It's very much me if you'll only remember."

"Do you have television?" he asked.

The question took her by surprise. "Yes, I do, up in my bedroom. Why?"

The drink was surging in her brain by now, encouraging her in fantasy. They would lie together on the bed upstairs, the bitterness of the years forgotten.

"And have you watched the news today?" he asked.

She nodded. "I saw that man's picture if that's what you mean."

He leaned forward, his face intense. "That man's name is John Raven. I want that bastard, Mildred. I want him in the worst way."

She barely heard him, resolved to be proven right or wrong. "Did you ever love me at all, Henry?"

The question stopped him in his tracks. "For Christ's sake, Mildred!" he expostulated. "Come on now! We had fun, didn't we? Wasn't that enough?"

"*Fun?*" she repeated. She looked at him with suddenly renewed hatred. "Is that how you think about it? Why did you come here, Henry?"

He shrugged, his face red and irritated. "I already told you. I'm in charge of this investigation. And we'd better get one thing straight, Mildred. It isn't you or me anymore. It's the law. A man has been murdered and I'm looking for his killer. I've got a good idea that you can help me."

Her laugh came close to hysteria. "Me? If you're talking about this man Raven, I never set eyes on him."

His charm had vanished completely. This was a man with no time to waste on niceties. He held up a Yale key between thumb and forefinger.

"Take a look at this. Have you ever seen it before?"

She took it in her hand. She shook her head. "Not as far as I know. Why? It's just an ordinary key, isn't it?"

"That's the one thing it isn't," he answered. "And don't fuck me around, Mildred. This key was found in George's house and Raven was looking for it. That much we know but he missed it. I want you to think of a lock it might fit, somewhere that George might have used as a hiding place."

"No," she said. The reply was really to all her dreams.

"Think," he urged. "Mildred, look at me!"

Her head came up very slowly. She saw herself in the mirror, a single tear furrowing her makeup.

"Please," he said. He spoke almost tenderly.

"You bastard," she said bitterly. "You've never had an ounce of real feeling in you. I'm glad you came. This way I can really be sure that you haven't changed. I don't know how I stood you as long as I did."

Hackett's face flushed but he made one last effort. "Mildred, listen to me. Don't have a man's death on your conscience."

The dam burst and the water ran fast and deep. She heard herself speaking above its noise.

"I'd like *two* men's deaths on my conscience. Yours would be the other one."

His eyes fixed her with frank contempt. "You raddled old bitch," he said balefully. "I'm going to make sure that you're taken care of."

The buttons were off the foils now but she had died once before. None of it mattered anymore. She came to her feet a little unsteadily.

"I want you to take your key and get out of here and never come back. And if you don't go I'll call the real police!"

He pursed his lips deliberately and spat. The spittle landed on her right cheek. She wiped it off mechanically, starting to laugh as she slammed the door behind him. Once alone, anger and revulsion took over. She heard him returning long before he reached the gate, willing him to ring the bell. The chimes sounded and she stood quite still, listening for the sound of his voice. When she heard it, she shot the bolts on the door. After a while, his footsteps retreated.

She poured herself another drink and sat down in front of the mirror, still scrubbing at her cheek. Raddled old bitch she may be but his eyes had told her the truth. Detective-Chief-Superintendent Hackett was a frightened man. He hadn't changed. He still tried to conceal his fear with aggression. The thought honed her hatred and she suddenly sensed that she had the power to destroy him. She didn't know how exactly but the clue was the key he had brought.

14

THE OPERATOR'S VOICE was briskly cheerful. "Good morning.
This is your wake-up call. It is exactly seven-fifteen."

He put the phone down on the floor by his head. He had
booked the call as insurance against oversleeping. He opened
a chink in the curtains. A plume of smoke rose above the brick
wall. The pub fires had already been lit. He let the curtain
fall back in place, yawning. Nature demanded her dues whatever the circumstances. A man had to sleep, eat, and drink.

He had found the way to keep the radiators working all
night and the studio was warm. He made tea and ate a slice
of bread and butter. By the time he had washed and shaved,
the eight o'clock signal was sounding in the transistor. He listened to the news as he dressed. Two announcers were making
the broadcast in tandem.

"And now," said one. "Over to Jack Bell at New Scotland
Yard."

Another voice assumed a tone of gravelly importance. "Here
is a police announcement. Members of the Western Robbery
Squad visited premises in Savernake Mews, Fulham, last night.
A man was found dead in what a police spokesman described
as suspicious circumstances. Police are anxious to trace the
whereabouts of a man called John Raven in connection with
their inquiries. Raven, aged forty-one, is six feet two and a
half inches tall. When last seen, he was wearing black leather
trousers, boots, and a nylon raincoat and hat. Anyone having
information about this man should communicate in confidence
with New Scotland Yard or the nearest police station. The
identity of the victim has not yet been revealed."

Raven switched off the set. He was almost relieved now that

he had heard the announcement. He had been waiting for it for something like thirty-six hours. They now had his bike and they had his description. He had to find fresh clothes and a new form of transportation. His picture could have been distributed to car rental firms and in any case he'd be asked for a driving license. He had to find an alternative.

He rummaged through the drawers and closets and found an armful of Louise Soo's winter sports clothes. He struggled into a Fair Isle sweater and pulled a gray wool cap low over his ears. He looked at himself in the mirror. It was better but the boots were still a giveaway. He cut them down to the ankles with a razor blade and shook his trousers over them. Then he stuffed the Smith and Wesson in his waistband and buttoned up the mac. It was a poor disguise but the best he could find at the moment.

A woman was mopping the pavement outside the pub, her back to him. A Labrador lying in a patch of pale sunshine lifted its tail as Raven walked away quickly. Garbage men were heaving cans into the back of their truck. He joined the line at the bus stop, changed to the Underground at Gloucester Road, and surfaced at Shepherd's Bush. He made his way to the open-air market. In spite of the early hour, business was brisk at some of the stands, the air around the Asian booths tangy with the smell of spices. A fat man, his face the color of his sausages, was selling wienies and frankfurters. Raven pushed through the crowd to Keglevic's store. The Pole was outside, taking down the protective grilles. He pulled Raven into the store hurriedly, locked the door, and reversed the sign so that from the street it read CLOSED. A radio was playing on the workbench.

Raven sat down. "You heard?"

Keglevic nodded. "Is on eight o'clock news. Those clothes, no good. I have something better. Why you don't call me last night?"

Raven spread his hands. "I had things to do." The cutdown

boots were chafing his ankles. He eased his legs tenderly.

"So what you do now?" The Pole poured coffee and passed a cup to Raven.

Raven managed a smile. It was typical of Keglevic that the question held no moral judgment.

"I was framed," he said. "And so was my girl. They planted drugs on us."

Keglevic swore as his own cup brimmed over. "Police frame you?"

"Yes." Raven's gaze was steady. "I didn't kill anyone, Jacek. I give you my word on it."

"Is a pity." The Pole's gold teeth gleamed. "Enemies are to be killed." He pulled a plastic bag from under the workbench. "For you. The Indians open for business half-past eight. I buy these things."

Inside the bag was a cheap corduroy suit, a shirt, tie, and raincoat. Raven put the bag on the floor.

"Why are you doing this, Jacek?"

The Pole threw the coffee dregs out of the back door. "Is for Casimir," he said, turning around. "Is for me. Is for all Poles you help in old times. You ask what you want, John, night and day. Now changing clothes!"

Raven stripped down to this shorts. The suit was a reasonable fit. He wiggled his toes.

"I'm going to need a pair of sneakers and some overalls."

The gun was on the bench next to Raven. Keglevic took it in his hand and spun the cylinder.

"Is heavy," he said. "You want, I get lighter."

"It'll do," said Raven. "Just the sneakers and overalls, please."

The street door clicked shut and Raven was alone in the store. His mind went back to Zaleski's funeral. It had been held at eleven o'clock at night with Raven the only non-Pole present. The side chapel had blazed with candles and flowers, a theater with the mourners performing a stylized drama. The coffin was open, Zaleski dressed in a new suit especially made for the occasion. His head rested on a red satin cushion. His monocle gleamed on his chest, attached to a silken cord. A trick of rigor mortis beyond the mortician's control had left his mouth set in a superior smile, as if he alone were above the emotions displayed by those who bent to kiss his cold cheek. Raven had taken his turn to embrace the dead man, feeling that he was saying goodbye to a whole way of life. The new generation of Poles was completely anglicized. But for exiles like Zaleski and Keglevic, there had never been a future, only a past.

Raven turned as the street door opened again. Keglevic was back carrying blue Bulldog overalls and a pair of sneakers.

"Size ten," said the Pole and dropped his purchases in Raven's lap.

Raven tied on the sneakers and scuffed dirt into the overalls. A couple of minutes' treatment gave them the appearance of use. He put the overalls in the plastic bag and stuffed the gun in his pocket. Keglevic was out in the yard, pouring kerosene over Raven's discarded clothing. Flames rose as he touched a match to the soaked pile. The Pole closed the back door and took a metal disk from a drawer. It was half an inch thick, an inch in diameter. He unscrewed the rim. Circuits were welded onto the copper base beneath the diaphragm. A tiny battery fitted into a slot at the side. The whole unit was secured by the screw-on rim.

Keglevic held the device in his bear's paw, grinning. "This for me!"

He handed Raven a tiny speaker no larger than a cigarette pack. "This for you!" He pointed at the switch on its base.

Raven thumbed it down. The room filled with a loud ticking, like the sound of a death-watch beetle magnified. Keglevic retreated backward through the yard door, still grinning, picking his way through the forest of twisted metal and plastic till he reached the wall thirty feet away. The ticking in Raven's hand was appreciably quieter. It increased in volume again as the Pole returned. Keglevic closed the door and leaned his back against it.

"So what you think?"

"It's brilliant," said Raven. The statement was no exaggeration. Transmitter and speaker could both be concealed in a shirt pocket. "What's the range? How far will the signal carry?"

The Pole juggled his enormous hands. "Is difficult to say. Three, four hundred yards. You wanted small so power is lost."

"It's great," said Raven. "Couldn't be better. Thank you, Jacek. How much do I owe you? This, the clothes, everything."

The Pole's eyes sought Raven's. "In times of troubles we are not speaking of money. Money is shit. Is necessary friends."

Raven nodded. "I'll be in touch, Jacek. And thanks again."

The Pole's strong embrace held Raven briefly. "Is always bed in the loft at Ealing. Day and night, remember. You telephone."

It was getting on toward ten o'clock. The street outside was crowded. Uniformed cops moved in pairs among Indian women in saris, Malays with wraparound skirts and flowers in their hair, West Africans in towering turbans. Chest-radios linked the police to their stations but none glanced twice at Raven. He bought pliers, tape, and a screwdriver in a hardware store, a newspaper from the stand at the end of the market. His photograph was on page three, next to an account of the police-court proceedings. The account linked his name with Kirstie's. The picture was ten years old and blurred. Raven dropped the paper in the nearest trash basket. He waited near the phone booths outside the station. It was exactly ten-thirty when he called the number Soo had given him. It was answered immediately.

"A Rover," said Soo. "Registration number TY two eight six five N. He's picking it up at the Pool."

Raven scribbled the number on the edge of a cigarette package. "Got it." He pushed the door ajar. It was hot in the booth. "Is there any news of Kirstie?"

"Patrick went to see her last night in Holloway. She's as cheerful as can be expected. He told her about you, John. He had to. In any case it's all over the newspapers. You don't want to reconsider?"

"There's nothing to reconsider," said Raven. "It's me, Jerry. That's all there is to it. Is there any chance of bail?"

"None," said Soo. "Patrick's going to Judge in Chambers but he hasn't got a chance."

In his heart Raven had never thought otherwise. The prosecution had a perfect case for holding Kirstie in custody. She was an alien who lived in France involved in a drugs case with a man wanted for murder. His mind shied away from the word. He put the phone down rather than enter into more dialogue. He had walked five yards when a hand touched his shoulder from behind. He paled, feeling the split-second tensing of muscles prepared for action. He turned as calmly as he could, prepared to run or to bluff.

The man was holding out Raven's cigarettes. "I believe these are yours," he said pleasantly.

Raven's smile creaked into place. He assumed a careless saunter that took him as far as the corner where he hailed a cab. He paid it off outside the Tate Gallery. He had a lot of time to kill and this was the best place to do it. For a man on the run it was perfect, a constantly shifting and changing crowd, places to eat and rest, telephones. He climbed the steps and checked the plastic bag containing the overalls. The corduroy suit was warm and his new shirt was sticking to his back. He bought a glass of lemonade in the cafeteria and took it to a table. A man and woman nearby were reading the same newspaper that he had bought. Raven could see his picture from where he sat. The man glanced at it casually, wet his thumb, and turned the page. Raven finished his drink. The public had been overexposed to pictures of I.R.A. bombers, mass-murderers, and rapists.

He moved constantly, going from room to room, from Turners to Stubbs to Surrealists, killing time and trying to ease the turmoil in his head. Kirstie had been right in a sense. He could have walked away from all this years ago. He could have bought a small boat and sailed around the world, lived without threat of danger. But people didn't really understand. They thought that he imagined himself as Captain Midnight. It just wasn't true. As far as he was concerned there was a right way to live and a wrong way. And if the wrong way was flaunted in his face, he reacted. It was as simple as that.

He made a meal of cold ham and salad and left the gallery at two o'clock. Everything would depend on the next few hours. If Hackett either didn't or couldn't supply the answer, then Raven was done for. He started walking toward the Byzantine spires and towers of Westminster Cathedral. The weak sun had dried nothing. Moisture seeped from the buildings and the grass was still wet. He was unable to get Kirstie out of his mind. He pictured her pacing the cell, afraid and bewildered with the utter loneliness of the innocent caught in a trap. And no one to talk to, that would be the worst of it. She knew now what had happened to him but rumor and fact would fuse in her brain. She'd read newspapers, hear other prisoners gossip. And at the end of the day, she would sleep behind bars, knowing that the man she shared her life with was being hunted for murder.

He turned right into Pimlico Parking and took the elevator to the top floor. He made sure that he was unobserved then started to make the tour of the floor. Halfway around he found what he was looking for, a Triumph Herald with the parking ticket displayed on the shelf above the dash. He could see the date-stamp. It was three days old and this was a long-term parking floor. He pried open a quarter-light with the screwdriver, pushed his arm through, and pulled up the door handle. Then he opened the choke and lifted the hood. He cut the ignition wires with the pliers, bared them, and touched the ends together. The motor fired but uncertainly. He taped the bare ends securely. The motor ground and fired again, this time on all four cylinders. He pushed in the choke. The motor was now running sweetly.

He switched the license plates with those on a nearby Datsun, pulled the overalls on top of his suit, and hid the gun under the driver's seat. Long-term parking could mean anything from a few days to months. He was gambling that the owner of the Triumph wouldn't try to claim his car while Raven was using it. And if he did, the police were going to be looking for a car bearing different plates. He felt his way into low gear and drove down the ramp. An Asian sitting in the exit booth took the ticket and Raven's money and raised the barrier. Raven headed the car toward Vauxhall Bridge. One across the river, he bought a box of spark plugs and a rotor arm. The salesclerk asked him if he wanted a bill.

"Yes," said Raven. "Make it out to the Metropolitan Police Motor Pool."

He slipped the bill under the wrappings on the package. It was dark by the time he turned the Triumph into the warren of access roads between Battersea Power Station, the Gas Works, and the British Rail Goods Depot. Railroad tracks crisscrossed the roads, the junctions were guarded by gates and signal boxes. There were no footpaths, just a waste of hardtop between functional buildings. He braked in front of a KEEP OUT sign, smashed a chain on a gate, and drove onto a badly lit lane. The lane led to an open space topped with cinders. An old railroad coach had been turned into a diner. It was strategically placed, drawing customers from the power station, gas works, Motor Pool, and the nearby fruit market. A line of refrigerated trucks was drawn up outside. Raven pulled the Triumph in behind a truck with Spanish registration and jump-stopped the motor.

The Motor Pool was immediately ahead. Raven remembered it well from the old days. Two big workshops backed on the river, with outside lamps lighting the hardtop out front. A concrete-block walk surrounded the Pool on three sides.

There was a gate with a guardhouse and an electric barrier for motor vehicles. The gun fitted snugly in a pocket of Raven's overalls, the magnetized transmitter in another. He walked as far as the diner. The move took him fifty yards closer to the Pool guardhouse. The diner was noisy and hot. A man and woman were dispensing food from behind the counter. Raven took his coffee to the window. He could see the guardhouse plainly now. Three cars were drawn up under the lights outside the workshops. It was impossible to read the numbers on the plates at this distance but one of the cars was a Rover V8.

He made his way outside and walked toward the checkpoint, carrying his package. The security guard was a man in his sixties. There was a phone on the shelf in front of him. He took his spectacles off as Raven arrived and slid the glass window back.

"What can I do for you, mate?" A finger held his place in the newspaper he was reading.

Raven placed the package on the shelf and took out the bill. "Spare parts. Some stuff for your stores." The man was reading yesterday's newspaper.

The security guard put his spectacles on again to inspect the bill. Then he ripped the cover off the box and looked inside.

"They're supposed to let me know who's coming," he grumbled. "That's the trouble with this bloody place, no communications. Do you know where to go?"

Raven shook his head. "First time." The box of parts was back in Raven's hands.

The guard leaned out of his booth, pointing toward the workshops. "See that door down there? Behind those cars? Just go through. Ask anyone where the stores are." He pulled his head back and closed the window.

Raven started walking toward the lights. Once behind the Rover he ducked low out of sight. The plates carried the right registration. The angle hid him from the guard sitting in the checkpoint. He was just about to clamp the transmitter under the Rover when the door opened. A mechanic threw out a bucket of water. Raven had a glimpse of cars up on hoists. There was a strong smell of paint. The mechanic looked at Raven curiously.

"Stores?" said Raven, holding up the package in his hand. He had a suspicion that the mechanic had seen him reaching under the Rover. The transmitter was back in his pocket. The next sequence of events came rapidly, heralded by a shout from the checkpoint. The security guard was out of his hut and coming toward the workshops, shouting as he advanced. "Hey you! Come back here!"

Raven put the Rover between the mechanic and himself. Two more security guards were crossing the workshop floor, heading for the door. He started to run. There was only one way to go, straight ahead. He pulled the gun from his pocket as he went. By the time he reached the booth, the white-faced guard was back behind the glass, the phone still off the hook in front of him. Raven was flying by now, past the barrier, his sneakers crunching into the cinders. He headed away from the lights into the safety of darkness, cannoning off obstacles but always running. He could smell the river. Stacks of timber loomed ahead. A dog lunged from the shadows, snarling on the end of a chain. Fifty yards more took him to a fence. He vaulted over it onto a grass embankment, railroad tracks below glinting in the light from a signal box. He crossed the tracks, climbed the grass on the opposite side, and negotiated another fence. He stripped off the overalls, hid them in a ditch and took his bearings. Battersea lay behind him, the river ahead. There was no question of going back to the Triumph. The alarm must have spread from the Pool. They'd be searching the diner, checking every vehicle parked in the area. The receiving end of Keglevic's device was on the passenger seat of the car. He stuffed the gun out of sight in his waistband and buttoned his jacket. There was a small rip in his trouser leg. Other than that he'd pass muster.

He started walking toward the river. More gates opened

onto the road. He could hear traffic passing on the other side. He unfastened the gates and found himself a couple of hundred yards from Chelsea Bridge. It was just after seven by his watch. He hurried over the bridge and flagged down a westbound cab on the other side. Twenty minutes later, he paid it off, a quarter mile away from the studios. He moved with the wiliness of the hunted man, avoiding open spaces, a sixth sense protecting his back. The lights from the pub spilled across the pavement. Nowhere had he ever felt safer than in this place at this moment. The chiming of the chapel clock broke the spell. He crossed the grass and let himself into the studio. No sooner had he poured himself a Scotch than the phone rang. He lifted the receiver, waiting until he heard Soo's voice before he answered.

"Something's come up," said Soo. "It may be important. Drake's ex-wife just called Patrick. She says she wants to see you. She says she has something that she thinks you might want. She refuses to talk to anyone else."

"Drake's *ex-wife?*" Raven sat down heavily.

His friend's tone was urgent. "Patrick says that she sounded in a real state, banging on about Hackett, what a shit he is and so forth. From what Patrick made out, she and Hackett had a fling together years ago."

Excitement coursed into Raven's bloodstream. "When was he there?"

"A little over an hour ago. Look, you're the one who's making the decisions, John. It's up to you. Anyway, here's the address."

Raven jotted it down. "I'm going out there, Jerry."

"Fair enough," said Soo. "There is something else. Patrick told me to tell you that he went to see Neil Suthern at the Home Office this afternoon."

Raven flicked an ash onto the newspaper. They were lining up behind him, risking their careers and reputations. Suthern was a close friend of Patrick's and assistant to the Permanent Minister of State.

"And?"

"He'll do whatever he can. I still think you're making a big mistake."

"It's a chance that I have to take," said Raven. "And by the way, I blew it at the Pool. The scheme I had didn't work."

Soo took the news philosophically. "I don't know what the hell you're up to but watch it whatever you do."

"I will," Raven said grimly. "How did Drake's wife manage to get hold of Patrick?"

"She read the report of Kirstie's trial and saw his name. She found his number in the book. Patrick thinks that she's genuine. Are you sure that you don't want him to go with you?"

"I'm sure," said Raven. He was sick of failure and running out of time. There was only one man who was right for what came next. "Can you be somewhere I can reach you for the rest of the evening?"

The answer came promptly. "I'll be at Kim's. If you can't call yourself, get someone else to do it but keep me informed. And listen, if you change your mind..."

"I won't change my mind," answered Raven. "And I won't forget who my friends are. I'll call you as soon as I can."

He made one more call, reaching Keglevic at his home. He told the Pole what had happened. "I'm sorry," he ended. "I left the transmitter in the car." Failure and apologies, he thought. He had to do better.

Keglevic roared like a bull. "Why be sorry? They trace it to me, I tell them. I fought for this bloody country! So where you want me to come?"

"There's a cinema on the corner of King's Road and Church Street. I'll be waiting inside. What car do you drive?"

"Is a Porsche. Old blue Porsche. I'll see you in twenty minutes."

Raven put the phone down. Instinct told him that this was his final commitment. He had no idea what was waiting at Forest Hill but he trusted his hunch. Drake, his ex-wife, and

Hackett. The combination *had* to produce what he needed. There was nowhere else left for him to go.

He left his gun in the studio and walked to the nearest bus stop. He no longer bothered with subterfuge, armed now with certainty. He left the bus on Beaufort Street and walked west. The blue Porsche was already waiting outside the cinema. The door on the passenger's side opened as Raven neared. He climbed in beside Keglevic. The Pole was a different man, elegant in gray flannel trousers and sports jacket and wearing spectacles, his mane tamed. He gave Raven his hand and grinned.

"Is like old times, John. You tell me where we go."

Something prompted Raven to open the glove compartment. Inside was a twenty-two revolver, pearl-handled and small enough to fit in a woman's purse.

Keglevic showed his gold teeth again. "Is Hanka's. From Poland."

Raven closed the glove compartment. "No more guns, Jacek. If this thing doesn't work out, I'm going to turn myself in."

Keglevic whipped off his spectacles and took a good look at Raven.

"I have to," said Raven. "I'll have gone as far as I can."

Whatever Keglevic saw seemed to satisfy him. He put his spectacles on again and started the motor.

"You are navigator. I am pilot. Let's go."

15

HE WENT DOWN the hill, carrying a cold kernel of fear in his stomach. He had played it all wrong. The bitch had been lying. He should have had the sense to give her whatever it was that she wanted. Apologies, promises, romance if he had to go the whole grisly way. Yet instead, he had spat in her face like some back-street whore.

He turned on impulse and retraced his steps. The lights were still on in the house. He lifted the gate latch and walked down the pathway. The chimes sounded loud in the hush. He heard the sitting room door being opened and pasted a smile on his face. The smile faded as the bolts were slammed home.

"Mildred?" he called but there was no reply.

He took a deep breath and walked back to the car, sure now that Mildred Drake held the answer to the key. He sensed it instinctively as well as the danger that it represented for him. He sat for a while thinking what he should do. Mildred might know where the key belonged but with luck she wouldn't know what he was looking for. Or would she? The possibility disturbed him deeply. His position had seemed so strong only yesterday when he'd been sure that the tape would be found in the bank. Now it was God knows where, to be picked up by some stranger, possibly, played out of curiosity.

His whole future hung on a throw of the dice. The threat now was double-edged. Raven was the only other person who knew the truth about Drake's death. For the first time, Hackett found himself thinking about hedging his bets. It was unbelievable. He could still walk into his office with the power to send people to jail, let others off the hook, yet a spool of magnetic tape and a man on the run could combine to destroy him.

There were certain things that had to be done as a matter of common sense. The first was to close his bank account, keep his money in cash. It would be easy to think of some excuse should the maneuver prove to have been unnecessary. And he'd need false identification. He ran a few names through his head, people he could lean on but it was all too haphazard. He used the radiophone to call his office. Most of the Squad had gone home for the night. Berger was acting as Duty

Officer. Commander Bolt had left a message that Hackett
was to call him at home. Hackett called in the number. Bolt
was in the middle of his evening meal and spoke with his
mouth full.

"I got your report. So the safe-deposit box was empty?"

"Except for the money, yes, sir." Hackett could hear women's
voices in the background.

"So we're back to square one." It was a conclusion that Bolt
clearly did not seem too pleased with.

"I'd say a whole lot better than that, sir. We're going to
get Raven, that's for sure." To gain time, he had to inspire
confidence.

Bolt grunted. "Well, I hope that you're right. Do you know
who I mean by Patrick O'Callaghan?"

"Yes, sir, I do. He's a friend of Raven's and Kirstie
Macfarlane's lawyer."

"And Neil Suthern? Does that name ring a bell?"

Hackett's mind slipped into higher gear. "I'm afraid not, no."

"Well, he's personal assistant to the Permanent Under Minister and happens to have been at school with O'Callaghan.
I'm told that they spent the best part of the afternoon
together."

Ice-cold water dripped into Hackett's veins. Bolt's tone was
peremptory. "Did you hear what I said?"

"I heard," said Hackett.

Bolt made his voice sharper. "There's no chance of this
Macfarlane prosecution backfiring, is there?"

"None at all," Hackett said stoutly. "I don't care who O'Callaghan knows, sir. This is one case that he's not going to win.
We've got the woman to rights and there is no defense."

"But in the meantime Raven's at large. And his friends are
opening doors that we don't want opened."

"We'll have him in forty-eight hours," promised Hackett.
The deadline gave him the time that he needed.

Bolt cleared his throat. "Well, I hope you get it right, Superintendent. Because it's your ass if you prove to be wrong.

As I told you, we're under political pressure. And try to be a little more accessible, will you! I want an up-to-date report of everything that's going on." The phone clattered down.

He was crossing Clapham Common when the red light glowed on the dash. Hackett pulled to the curb and picked up the phone again. The voice had an unnatural huskiness as if the caller were attempting to disguise it.

"Is that Henry Hackett?"

"Speaking," said Hackett.

"You don't know me," said the voice. "But we're on the same side. You could be in trouble. C11 just pulled your file."

The phone went dead. Hackett put the receiver down as if it were loaded with explosive. The lights shone like diamonds across the lonely stretches of turf outside. Instinct told him that the call was no hoax. The two events were linked together, O'Callaghan's visit to the Home Office and the anonymous tip-off. Bolt's concern had been entirely for himself. There'd been no hint that he knew any more than he said. But this meant little. A confidential message passed at ministerial level would be way above Bolt's head.

He drove back to the Yard, parked, and went into the building. He crossed the Central Hall looking neither right nor left. Upstairs in his office he locked the door, a badly shaken man. Just one false step and he could be in Raven's position. He started clearing his desk of personal papers, feeding them into the shredding machine that stood in the corner. He worked quickly, ignoring the ringing of the two telephones. He unlocked the door, carrying a briefcase containing his checkbook and passport. The outer office was empty and stank of tobacco smoke. The cleaners had not yet been in. He cut the lights and let himself out into the corridor. Every greeting represented a possible menace. C11 recruited people from other squads, sleepers who stayed at their jobs until the time came for them to surface with whatever information they had gleaned. Hackett's mind was running on flight now and for that he needed help.

It was getting on toward nine o'clock when Hackett parked in Soho. The decision he had just made would affect his whole life. The rope was getting shorter all the time. Strobe and strip lighting leaked color onto the pavements. Blinking signs offered nude dancers and models (cameras supplied). Pockmarked touts beckoned from tawdry foyers where bump-and-grind music played. Spitted ducks, looking as though they had been varnished, revolved in the windows of Chinese restaurants. A few bums sat in doorways, empty cider bottles behind them, dirty hands soliciting alms. But this was a street without charity. Sex, food, and entertainment were strictly for profit.

Hackett climbed the two flights of stairs and pressed the doorbell, eyeing the television camera set in the ceiling. The usual interval passed before the door was opened by the crop-haired Chinese man in the mohair tunic. Silk curtains were drawn in Lam Po Hong's room. The indirect lighting softened outlines of the jade figures and porcelain. Lam Po Hong was standing with his back to the window, bland, squat, and impressive in a well-cut business suit. The sound of music drifted up from the penny arcade below.

The servant closed the door from the outside. "I had to see you," Hackett blurted out. "I couldn't trust the phone. I got the tip half an hour ago. It's all over."

The Chinese man opened a black lacquer cabinet. The lining was refrigerated. He took out a half-bottle of champagne. The cork hit the ceiling. He was quick with the glass, catching the bubbling liquid and handing the drink to Hackett.

"Sit down," he said quietly. "What is all over?"

"The jig's up," said Hackett. "I'm about to be investigated. I don't know how good a case they'll have but I don't intend to stick around and find out. I'm leaving the country, Hong, and I need your help."

Hong took a seat, his face expressionless. "Does anyone else know that you're here?"

The bubbles exploded on Hackett's palate. If Hong knew

about the tape, that his name figured on it, Hackett would be dead before he reached his car, his body bundled into a sack and sunk without trace.

He raised his head. "Only one person knows where I am, the man who tipped me off. Look, you're in the clear. I'm the one in the shit. And if the worst came to the worst you know that I wouldn't testify. I couldn't afford to, could I?"

Hong's smile was delicate. "It's a peculiar way of putting it but I understand what you mean."

Hackett put his empty glass down and lit a cigarette nervously. "You've got to do your share. You've got to help me."

Hong nodded slowly. "How much time do you think you have?"

Hackett spread his hands. "There's no way of telling. The investigation's only just gone into the pipeline. I just left my office. It looks as if I'm clean at the moment but there's no telling when the action could start."

Hong refilled Hackett's glass. "And if you stay and face the investigation?"

Hackett drew a finger across his windpipe. "I'd be dead. I'd have no chance. This is Criminal Investigation. These people don't start anything that they can't finish."

Hong opened a drawer then closed it again. "Do you have money?"

"As soon as the banks open in the morning," said Hackett. "What I need is to be landed in Holland with a passport that'll stand scrutiny."

Hong spoke into the voice-box in front of him, firing rapid Cantonese. He opened the drawer again.

"Have you been back home?"

"Not yet," said Hackett. The prospect seemed more hazardous as time went on.

"Is there anything there that you need?"

Hackett shook his head. "Not really, no."

Hong slid a key across the desk. "Then don't go back there.

This house belongs to a friend. Put your car in the garage and go to bed. And no more visits here, no more phone calls. Is that understood?"

"Understood," said Hackett. The address on the label attached to the key was in Teddington. *Range Cottage, Weir Road.*

"It's near the lock," smiled Hong. Now that he was concerned, he made everything sound reasonable. "Relax. By this time tomorrow you'll be in Amsterdam." He pushed out his hand.

Hackett rose and took it. Hong's palm was warm and dry like the skin of a reptile.

"So how do we do it?" asked Hackett. "You come and collect me or what?"

"Someone will come and collect you," said Hong. "You can have complete confidence. And remember, no phone calls here. Goodbye, Mr. Hackett. Loyalty must always be rewarded."

The Rover was parked near the entrance to an open-air lot at the end of Gerrard Street. Hackett sat behind the wheel, watching the second-story windows of the building he had just left. After a few minutes the lights went out. Hong's exit was conducted with military precision. A couple of men emerged, blocking off the street on both sides as a black Mercedes drew up. Someone in the car opened the rear door and Hong hurried across the pavement. Seconds later there was neither sign of car nor bodyguard.

Hackett drove over the cinders onto the street. He found the location he needed on the map. It was a straggling street with houses on one side facing the sodden meadows on the south bank of the river. Beyond the towpath and weir, a footbridge led to the lights of Teddington. Hackett drove slowly, headlights picking out the shingles fixed to the walls and gates. Driveways disappeared into tangles of trees and bushes, the houses hidden from sight. Toward the end of the street, four bare chestnut trees showed up ahead. Two gates bore the name of the bungalow. Hackett stopped the car. There was no sign of life anywhere. The street lights shone on desolate stretches of sidewalk. Trees creaked in the wind. He unfastened the gate and turned in between laurel bushes dripping with mist from the river. The hardtop was pitted with potholes. He continued through a spinney of willow trees warped by the wind to a clearing in front of the block-built bungalow. The powerful headlights lit the front of the building like a stage set. There were four windows, each protected on the inside by a steel shutter.

Hackett cut the motor. Pools of stagnant water blocked drains. The flowerbeds were unkempt and uncared for. He tried the garage. It was locked. He walked back to the front door. If there were lights in the neighboring houses he could not see them. The mat in front of the door was littered with fallen leaves. He used the key that Hong had given him and stepped into the small hallway. The bungalow was completely still, the musty air trapped by the steel shutters. He kicked the door shut and turned on the lights. The head of a wild boar glared from the wall. A set of car keys hung from one of its tusks. He switched on more lights. The hallway led directly to the heart of the bungalow, an oblong sitting room with access to kitchen and bedroom. The steel shutters were fitted throughout, hinged to the wall, and secured with bolts. A door from the kitchen opened into the two-car garage. Light from the overhead bulb shone on a Japanese pickup. He moved the Rover in beside it, locked the connecting door, and went back into the sitting room. A telephone bill on the table was addressed to Mr. Lee Chan. It was ten days old.

The furniture, the double bed, sofa, and chairs were adequate for a weekend cottage or summer home. There was a color television set, a couple of shelves filled with books covering aspects of big-game hunting, and a picture of a Chinese in a deerstalker hat and camouflage jacket standing next to a dead stag. Hackett went into the bedroom. The clothes closet and drawers were empty except for a few articles of men's clothing. There was no sign of a woman's presence. There were no sheets on the bed. He found a store of linen in a cupboard next to the hot-water tank, made the bed, and turned on the two-bar heater. He left the lights on as he moved from room to room. The shutters made it impossible to see a yard otherwise. The refrigerator in the kitchen was empty except for a bottle of stale milk and some dubious-looking sausages. But he found food in a well-stocked cupboard, tea, cheese, canned milk, and crackers. He carried the tray into the sitting room.

He was halfway through his meal when he noticed something under the sofa. He went down on his knees. There were two wooden gun-cases. The first held a Winchester pump gun. The second was lined. Fitted snugly in the mock velvet was a Czech deer rifle with telescopic sights. Hackett weighted both weapons, thoughtfully. Steel shutters and guns like this, a man could handle most situations. He pushed the gun-cases back under the sofa and looked for ammunition. He found it in a drawer in the telephone table. A box of twelve-bore cartridges for the shotgun and fifty shells for the deer rifle.

He finished his crackers and cheese, speculating about Lee Chan. The man was clearly a hunter, someone who took good care of his weapons. The barrels were clean and oiled, the walnut stocks polished. He lit a cigar and inspected the picture again. After eleven years on the Drugs Squad he recognized an Oriental as readily as a Westerner. The man in the photograph was a stranger.

He took the tray out to the kitchen. There was a bottle of gin on the counter but no tonic. He found ice cubes and opened a can of grapefruit juice. The mixture was drinkable. Back in the sitting room, he switched on the television set, switching off again before the picture even formed on the screen. He was unable to concentrate, his mind on other things. He'd managed to push Drake's death to the back of his consciousness. If he thought of it at all, it was with resentment. The bastard had brought it on himself. Hackett's animosity pitched on Mildred, but the problem now was C11.

He jumped as the phone rang, rattled by the unexpectedness of its summons. He let it ring for some time before answering. It was Hong. Hong's voice was quietly reassuring.

"Is everything all right out there?"

"Yes," said Hackett. He was gradually picking up the sounds of the bungalow, an occasional scurry in the rafters, the singing of the alders outside. He had opened one of the shutters in the kitchen.

"You're quite sure that nobody followed you? It's important."

"I'm sure," said Hackett. It was the one thing that he could be certain about.

"Good," said Hong. "Well now listen! You are not to go anywhere near Bulstrode Street. *Under no circumstances*! Is that understood?"

Hackett's pulse accelerated. As far as he knew Hong had never had his home address. Hackett's voice was strained.

"Yes, but can't you tell me why?"

"I can," said Hong. "There's a police car sitting outside your apartment building. Stay where you are. Don't move. All the necessary arrangements have been made. You'll be out of the country by tomorrow evening."

A thought hit Hackett like a hammer. He ground his dead cigar into the ashtray.

"But they know where I bank! They'll be waiting. I've got to get money from somewhere."

Hong's voice was confident. "Relax, Mr. Hackett. Everything's going to be taken care of. You've done your part, now I am doing mine. There'll be a place for you somewhere. Don't worry, we'll find it. Just stay put and relax. I'll call you at noon."

Hackett's thoughts returned to the voice that had warned him earlier. Clearly it had been disguised. He knew better

than anyone that what little popularity he had extended no
further than his own Squad. And none of them could have access to the information his caller had given. It had to be someone in a key position; someone who would know that his file
had been pulled; someone with a stake in Hackett's survival.
Another voice sounded in his mind, bland and reassuring. His
brain focused sharply and he emptied his lungs of cigar
smoke. *It was Hong!* Of course, it was Hong! The voice belonged to someone on Hong's payroll who had made his report and been told what to do. This had to be the answer. It
would explain Hong's lack of alarm, his readiness to help.

Hackett's fingers found his nose. The slant-eyed monkey!
He'd sat there in his room, surrounded by all that jade and
stuff, looking like some kind of idol, listening to what he already knew and planning each move as a chess player does.

Hackett's cigar had gone out again. He relighted it and
poured himself another drink, assessing his new position. It
was stronger than he could have hoped for given the circumstances. It was Hong who had the interest in Hackett's survival.

He sat there, mulling over what Hong had said. *There'll be
a place for you somewhere.* You bet there would. If he only
had the tape, it could be his passport to fortune. His own involvement no longer mattered once he was safely out of the
country, but Hong's operations would be finished in England.

He smiled for the first time in hours and looked at his
watch. Ten past eleven. This time he wouldn't blow it. Memories that were almost forgotten shaped his approach. He finished his drink, lit his last cigar, and sat at the telephone. His
fingers were shaking as he dialed the number. God alone knew
that it was going to be difficult but somehow he had to keep
the balls in the air.

He heard the click as the line opened, her breathing as she
held the mouthpiece close.

"Who is it?"

"Don't hang up," he said quickly. "Whatever you do, don't

hang up. Please listen to what I have to say."

"I'm listening," she said. Her voice was quiet. There was none of the drunken abuse he'd expected.

He tried to match her mood, striving for the note of sincerity. "I've been sitting here for the last two hours, trying to crank up the courage to call you. And now the words won't come."

"What is it you want?" she asked. "Do you want to apologize for spitting in my face, for calling me a raddled old bitch?"

He reached for her over the length of cable. "I loved you, Mildred. I suppose I still love you. I can only say that I never felt the same about anyone else. All the other things are just part of it. Anger, bitterness, all the insults."

"A strange way of showing love," she said coolly.

Her face appeared in the ensuing silence, her eyes searching his. "It's too late for us to lie," he said. "We need one another."

"Do we?" she countered. "Or is it that *you* need *me*? Isn't that the formula, Henry?"

A car stopped outside, backed through the open gateway, and drove off in the opposite direction.

"We need one another," he said obstinately.

She broke the silence again. "You can't go through life caring about nobody but yourself without paying the price. It might be a long time before the bill comes in but sooner or later you have to pay it."

He took a quick sip of the gin and grapefruit juice. "I'm paying it now. I'm in bad trouble, Mildred, and you're the only one who can help me." It was a deliberate gamble but he figured that the odds were shaded in his favor.

Her voice was gentle. "Tell me how I can help you, Henry."

Her answer gave him new hope. He had never offered a hand that she had not finally accepted.

"That key," he said. "The one I showed you tonight. I was lying to you. It had nothing to do with George's death."

"I know," she said. "You see, while you were sitting down trying to find the nerve to call me, I was destroying you, Henry. I was breaking you up in small pieces and feeding you to the fishes."

"I don't understand what you're talking about," he said cautiously. She was definitely unhinged, drunk or not.

"But I *want* you to understand!" her voice seemed to dance with enthusiasm. "I'm talking about revenge. You know, scratch a lover and find an enemy! I just came back from the Home Office. Would you like to know who took me there?"

He knew the answer already but forced himself to listen. "Who?"

"John Raven and his solicitor. I lied too, Henry. The key you showed me belonged to the garage. I had the second one. We found what you were looking for."

The knuckles on his clenched fist were white. Everything he had feared had come true.

"You stinking rotten bitch!" he said bitterly.

She laughed almost merrily. "That's more like the real Henry Hackett! God, what a shit you are! I wonder how it's possible for someone like you to breathe the same air as other people!"

He pictured the triumph on her face. Cold rage flooded into his mind, pointing it at the gun-cases under the sofa. Drake was already dead. A single shot would send her to join him. His voice was barely audible.

"O.K., you win. But I knew you always would. Could I see you one last time?" He held his breath as if breathing might betray his real purpose.

The suggestion seemed to amuse her. "Is that what you'd really like to do, Henry?"

He was no longer sure of her. "It's all I have left," he said. There was no real need to confront her. A shot in the dark at a window would do the trick. He could be at Forest Hill before she went to bed. Two killings were no worse than one and he'd be out of the country before her body was found.

She was still on the line, almost supercilious in her assurance. "I'd ask you here but I'm waiting for a taxi. Mr. O'Callaghan insisted that I spent the night in a hotel. I got the impression that he was worried about you. You see, I told them everything. But I've got another idea. If you want to finish in style, join the party on Mr. Raven's houseboat, tomorrow night at seven. You'll see a lot of familiar faces."

He slammed the phone down, the force of his gesture chipping the mouthpiece. He might have to bide his time but sooner or later she'd learn what vengeance meant. He hung his clothes carefully, cut the lights, and crawled into bed.

He woke, confused and disoriented. The darkness was complete. He groped for the bedside lamp, yawning. Memories flooded back. The most bitter was that of Mildred. Her betrayal had been deliberate. She could have helped him, taken him by the hand, and led him to the garage or she could have sat tight and said nothing at all to anyone. But no, she'd settled for nothing less than his total destruction. Only it wasn't going to work like that. He might not have the tape but he still had Hong.

He pulled on his trousers and went into the kitchen. Gray light shafted between the open steel shutters. The trees outside bore their gray November look, cheerless and miserable. The flowerbeds and driveway were littered with fallen leaves. An electric milk-cart floated by as he watched. Used as he was to the bustle of his own neighborhood, he felt an eerie stillness about this street. There was no sign of life at all. No children, no dogs, nothing but trees, bushes, and hidden houses. There had been no rain during the night but the road and driveway were wet. He made himself some sort of breakfast. The taste in his mouth was foul. There was no razor or toothbrush in the bathroom. He did the best he could with his finger, salt, and warm water then put on the rest of his clothes. His car radio wouldn't work in the garage and he couldn't find a set in the bungalow. The first television newscast was at one o'clock. He washed up the breakfast things, taking his time. The waiting was the worst of all.

His mind dragged back yet again to Mildred Drake. He pulled one of the gun-cases from under the sofa and sat with the deer rifle across his knees. It was Finnish, a Tikka 270, and beautifully machined, the scope sight a miracle of modern technique. He took a shell from the box and slotted it into the breech. Then he carried the gun into the kitchen. Low-lying meadows stretched away to the river. A couple of hairy-hocked ponies were grazing near the fence, a hundred and fifty yards away. He opened the back door on impulse. Heavy duty cardboard boxes were piled at the rear of the garage, stained and ravaged by rain. The stenciled address on them read Ho Chang c/o Mandarin Trading Company, Gerrard Street W.1. A blackbird scuttled under a bush with a call of alarm as Hackett made his way to the end of the garden. Dense privet hedges, unpruned and overgrown, made impenetrable barriers on each side. There was no one to watch as Hackett rested the rifle on a post. He could see the gypsy encampment close to the weir, an old motorized caravan and a horse-drawn cart. Lines of washing had been strung between the two vehicles and a curl of smoke rose from the caravan stack.

The ponies had their heads down, grazing. Hackett drew a bead on the one that was nearer, aiming at a point below and in front of its withers. Caprice prolonged its life for a few more seconds as the animal sniffed at a clump of dockweed and then moved on a couple of yards. Hackett settled his shoulder firmly into the butt and squeezed the trigger. The report was sharp but without much volume. The pony keeled over, kicked, and lay still. Its mate continued to graze, undisturbed. White smoke drifted above Hackett's head. The smell of the exploded shell was acrid. He waited, hidden by the hedge, but there was no indication that the gunshot had been heard or noticed. He ejected the shell and heeled it into a flowerbed. The episode left him with a feeling of intense satisfaction. Tension had left his body and mind. He thought no more of the animal's death than he had of Drake's. His only regret on this occasion was that it hadn't been Mildred in his sights.

He closed and locked the back door and cleaned the rifle carefully, using the ramrod and rag. That done he smoked one of the butts in the ashtray. He thought of exploring the neighborhood, finding a store that would supply tobacco and razors. Then he imagined Hong calling while he was out. He picked up the phone, making sure that it was working. The morning dragged on. It was after eleven when he heard wheels turning onto the driveway. He moved quickly to the kitchen and stationed himself behind the shutters. A red P.O. van pulled up in front of the door. A postman clambered out and rang the doorbell. Hackett stayed where he was. The bell rang a second time then the mail flap was lifted. The van drove off. A card lying in the hallway said that an attempt had been made to deliver a package that could be retrieved at the local post office.

At noon, he was standing at the kitchen window, his eyes on the driveway, his ears clamped to the telephone. The minutes crawled by. Twelve-thirty, one o'clock. At one-fifteen he picked up the phone and called Hong's office. Someone picked up.

"Mr. Hong," said Hackett. "I'd like to speak to Mr. Hong, please."

He heard the phone being replaced at the other end. Hackett redialed. This time there was no answer. Anxiety flooded into his mind. The hunt would be well and truly on by now. The ranks always closed on scandal. There'd be no general alarm inside Scotland Yard but the chase would be no less intense. He pictured the confusion in his own office. Meade would be running around like a lost dog, Bolt backing away, his hands held high, denying anything that might involve him.

Hackett knew every move. C11 would have their own men at the ports, they wouldn't put their faith in the Special Branch. Hackett's bank would have been alerted. One check cashed with a bank card would send the teleprinter tapping furiously.

He poured himself a glass of the flat tasteless water, sensing the first real experience of panic. Even the use of the Rover would be dangerous. C11 would know that he'd drawn a vehicle from the Pool. Suddenly he thought of the pickup. He collected the ignition keys from the tusk in the hallway. There was a trilby in one of the sitting room closets. He grabbed it and went out to the garage. The registration on the Datsun was valid. He retrieved his gun from the glove compartment in the Rover and opened the garage doors. Then he settled himself behind the wheel of the pickup. The motor fired immediately. He drove out, locked up behind him, and headed for the bridge.

It was after two in Chinatown. He used the short cuts from the parking lot to Gerrard Street, the collar of his overcoat turned up, the trilby as low on his head as he could get it. He reached the top of the second flight of stairs before realizing that something was wrong. The television camera was still angled in the ceiling but the plate on the mahogany door had been removed, the screw-holes filled in and painted over. He put his finger on the bell. A Chinese woman opened the door, a woman he had never seen before. She was tiny and wore a black cotton top and trousers.

"Mr. Hong," said Hackett. "I'd like to speak to Mr. Hong, please. I'm a friend."

She positioned herself so that he could not see past her. Her face was like a withered russet and most of her teeth were missing.

"Mistah Hong not here. Mistah Hong in Singahpore."

Hackett thrust out a foot, preventing the door from closing. "Look, who else is here? I need to talk to someone. Did Hong leave a message?"

She crossed her arms over her chest, her eyes resigned, and made no reply. He pushed past her quickly and opened doors along the passage. Hong's room had been stripped of its elegance, the jade and silk tapestries gone. The other rooms were furnished as offices. These too had been denuded of everything except basic equipment. There was a kitchen at the end of the passage. There was no one there either, no food, nothing but a sleeping bag on the floor.

He ran down the stairs and hurried back to the Datsun, picking up something to smoke on the way. The stubble on his face was forgotten. The bungalow was just as he had left it. He put the pickup in the garage and let himself into the kitchen. He could see the dead pony lying in the field, the second animal grazing a hundred yards away.

He slumped down on the sofa, staring down at the case that contained the deer rifle. Everything was closing in on him, every hand he touched betrayed him. That bitch had finally beaten him. There was nowhere left for him to go, nowhere to run to. He took the rifle out of the case and placed it across his knees. One shot and it would all be over. All it needed was the strength to take himself out and death would cancel everything.

A surge of hatred gave him fresh direction. She'd stripped him of everything. Even his fear belonged to her. It was she who'd created it, nurtured it, and then winged it into his brain like a poisoned dart. If it had to end this way, he would take her with him.

16

THE PORSCHE stopped halfway up the hill and both men un-
wound themselves. All the lights were on in the house. They
could hear the music playing from where they were across the
street. Keglevic reached into the glove compartment. His hand
came out holding his tiny gun. He shook his head.

"Is better," he said.

Raven's sneakers made no sound as they walked down the
paved pathway. The curtains were drawn and it was impossible to see into the house. An overflowing garbage can and
a row of unwashed milk bottles stood outside the porch. Raven
pressed the bell. Chimes sounded inside. After a while, a
woman spoke from the hallway, her voice slurred.

"Who is it?"

The two men exchanged glances. "Trouble," Raven said
quietly, and then louder, "You asked me to come here!"

"Just a minute!" The door opened on a short length of chain.
A woman was staring at him with greenish eyes set in a dead-
white face. Her auburn hair fell to her shoulders and she wore
a clinging black dress, platform shoes, and a ratty-looking fur
jacket around her shoulders. "I told the lawyer, I don't want
to see anyone else but you. Nobody!" Her eyes were on Keglevic. She must have been fifty and her teeth were too good
to be true.

"If you see me, you see him," said Raven. "That's the way
it has to be."

She took the chain off the door. "Then make him put that
gun away. I know who you are. Your picture was on television."

Keglevic dropped the gun in his jacket pocket. The two men

followed her into the hallway. She shut the door and bolted it behind them. The furniture in the sitting room was as bizarre as its owner, Tottenham Court Road chairs, gate-leg table, and an ugly Victorian bureau. The once white Chinese carpet was covered with drink stains. Keglevic's enormous hand gently removed the glass from Mildred Drake's grasp. She whirled like a tigress, eyes blazing, and snatched the glass back.

"Don't you ever do that again!" she warned. "Do you understand?"

Keglevic made a courtly gesture, his hand on his heart. "O.K."

She took another swig from the whisky glass and considered them both from under her long false eyelashes.

"Can you dance?" she asked suddenly.

Raven's heart sank. This was going to turn out to be some ghastly hoax by a drunken maniac. Keglevic showed a bank of gold teeth.

"Waltz," he said, "mazurka, and foxtrot."

She smiled dreamily as if at some distant memory. "I used to be the best dancer at the Hammersmith Palais-de-Danse. That was before I was married. All the girls were jealous of me." She sat down unsteadily.

Raven switched off the record player. Then he squatted down in front of her, holding her thin wrists. Her pulse fluttered erratically.

"Listen to me, Mrs. Drake. I'm in bad trouble. You told Patrick O'Callaghan that you could help me."

"Help you," she said, the loose skin at the bottom of her neck quivering.

He tried again. He had to get through to her somehow. "Hackett was here. Do you remember that, Mrs. Drake?"

She nodded slowly, her eyes searching his. Her hands had neither weight nor resistance. "He came with the key."

"What key was that?" Raven's tone was gentle.

Her mouth was bitter. "Christ, how I hate that bastard!"

The tears came fast, collecting mascara on the way and furrowing through the thick makeup.

He took the frail wrists again, forcing her to look down at him. Keglevic was sitting bolt upright like some spellbound theatergoer.

"You said you could help," prompted Raven.

Her tears were still flowing. "Those two men destroyed my life between them."

"Keep your eye on her," Raven said to the Pole. He found an espresso machine in the kitchen and brewed a cup of strong hot coffee. She drank it like a child, weeping and hiccoughing. They watched in silence as she made an effort to pull herself together.

"Listen to me," Raven said finally. "I'm the man who sent your husband to prison. He came out with one thing in mind, to destroy me. He and Hackett were in it together. They framed me, planted dope on my boat."

Her eyes were beginning to focus. "Did you kill George? That's what Hackett said, that you killed George."

"He was dead when I found him," said Raven. "Hackett killed him."

Her face creaked into a smile. "Beautiful!" The smile became a laugh and she choked, covering her mouth with a lace-edged handkerchief. She dabbed at her eyes and finished the rest of her coffee.

Raven pleaded with her. "It's the end of the line for me unless you help me."

She looked into the palm of her hand and then touched his cheek with it.

"I'll help you. I'll tell you why Hackett was here." She pulled herself erect and went to the bureau. She turned, holding up a Yale key in her fingers. "This is why he came. He had a key like this. He wanted to know where it belonged."

Raven's tone was that of someone who soothes a frightened animal. "Do *you* know where it belongs?"

She moved her head. "Yes, but I didn't tell him."

Raven spoke quietly. "Will you tell me, Mrs. Drake?"

Her eyes studied his face before she replied. "There's a locked garage at the top of the hill. It belongs to the house. When George left, I let it to neighbors. There were three keys. George had one, the boy who rents it has one, and I have the other."

"Will you take me there?" asked Raven. He could hear Keglevic's loud breathing.

"Yes," she said quickly. "Just let me put my face on." They waited as she found her purse and repaired her makeup. There was little sign left of her drunkenness when she had finished. "Ready," she said briskly and wrapped her fur tighter around her shoulders.

She picked up a flashlight in the hallway. They walked up the hill, Keglevic on one side of her, Raven on the other. Her mind seemed to have cleared and she chatted away as they climbed. The hill ended in an oblong of hardtop, flanked on one side by a row of garages. Railings and a gate showed an entrance to the park opposite. The clouds overhead were ragged. An occasional glimpse of a crescent of moon showed through the rents. Mildred Drake led the way across and stopped in front of a door.

"This one," she said and gave Raven the key.

He raised the weighted door and found the light switch. Underneath the naked bulb was a small sports car with the top down. Keglevic lowered the door. He had said very little since arriving in Forest Hill, seemingly fascinated by Mildred Drake. The bulb was dusty, the light poor. Her face was almost girlish. She must have been aware of the Pole's interest and giggled.

"Isn't this exciting! What are we looking for?"

Raven's glance took in the walls and the workbench. He didn't know the answer to her question but he was sure of one thing. If they found whatever it was, it would be the last piece in the puzzle, the piece that Hackett had been prepared to kill for. Raven moved the flashlight, exploring the walls in search of loose masonry but the mortar was old and hard. There was no inspection pit in the concrete floor. He turned his attention to the rafters, climbing up on the workbench to get a better view. The beam traveled along the dusty ledge and suddenly stopped. He thrust his hand into the far recess and touched something that was wrapped in plastic. He pulled out a small cassette player. He clambered down, forgetting the pain in his legs. Keglevic and Mildred Drake watched with open curiosity as Raven placed the cassette player on the front end of the convertible.

"This is what Hackett was looking for." There was a blend of triumph and certainty in Raven's voice. He switched on the player. They stood in silence, listening as the recital began.

They heard one side through, Mildred Drake's hand covering her mouth, Keglevic's eyebrows bent in a frown. Raven turned off the set.

Keglevic shook his head. "Bloody hell!"

Raven put the set in his pocket. "Let's get back to the house," he said quietly.

He replayed the tape in the sitting room, the names and voices he knew and those that were strange to him evincing a tale of conspiracy and graft that went back nine years. The last part of the reverse side of the spool proved the clincher. Hackett's and Drake's voices took them step by step through the plot to frame Raven and Kirstie Macfarlane. A background of chinking crockery suggested a restaurant.

Raven's voice broke the sudden silence. "Where's your phone?"

She took him upstairs. There was a stuffed hippopotamus on the bed. The covers had been turned down on clean sheets sprigged with a flower design. Raven dialed his lawyer's number, his words stumbling with excitement.

"You'd better get hold of your friend, Patrick. We've just

hit the jackpot." He explained what had happened.

O'Callaghan's reaction was prompt. "Who else is there with you?"

"Just Keglevic and Mrs. Drake."

"Then here's what you do. Get out of that house straight away. I'll contact Soo. Just get in your car and bring Mrs. Drake straight to my office. Now move!"

Raven went downstairs. Mildred was giggling, showing Keglevic a photograph album. Raven took it away from her.

"Get yourself a proper coat," he said. "We're going out!"

Her eyes were lively, as though her life had acquired new meaning. She flashed them both a smile and went upstairs. Raven looked across at his friend.

"Will you drive me to my lawyer's place?"

Keglevic shrugged. "Why asking? We are together."

"I don't know how this is going to work out," Raven warned. "I can only hope. I can't be certain. But if there's going to be any shit I want you out of it."

Keglevic made no reply. He was on his feet, standing as Mildred Drake came back into the room. She was wearing a belted brown coat.

"I'm ready," she said brightly.

Raven turned the lights off and made sure that she had her house keys. The rear seats in the Porsche were made for dwarfs or children. Mildred Drake sat sideways, her long legs tucked up under her, one hand trailing over the driver's seat close to Keglevic's shoulder. By the time they reached the bottom of the hill, she was humming.

Lights shone in the house on Upper Berkeley Street. Keglevic parked outside. The door opened as they crossed the street. Patrick O'Callaghan was waiting in the hallway, his bow tie askew. A quick glance took in Keglevic and Mildred, then he checked the street and closed the door.

"Upstairs," he said, pointing at the lighted doorway on the second floor.

There was no sign on the door. A reception area with a

couch and magazine rack led to an office with desks and type-writers. Beyond this was the lawyer's room, dominated by a life-size statue of Saint Francis carved in wood and painted. The top of the desk looked as if every drawer had been removed and emptied out on it. Piles of legal documents tied with pink tape stood knee-high on the floor. A stained and battered trilby hung from a light fixture.

A short dark man in a dinner jacket and cummerbund was sitting behind the desk. O'Callaghan made the introductions.

"Neil Suthern — John Raven, Mildred Drake and..." He hesitated.

"Keglevic!" The Pole bowed.

The lawyer found chairs. "Neil's from the Home Office."

Raven pulled the cassette player from his pocket. "Hackett was at Mrs. Drake's house tonight, looking for this. You'll hear why."

He put the player down on the desk. They heard both sides of the tape in silence, O'Callaghan making notes. Suthern held out his hand. Raven pushed the set across the desk. Suthern's question was for Mildred Drake.

"Are you prepared to make a statement that Hackett came to your home tonight?"

She was sitting in the pose of an early Bacall. Coat collar up and belt drawn in tightly. One leg was crossed over the other and swinging.

"I'd be delighted," she said.

Suthern's glance switched to the lawyer. "We've got quite enough here. I'll try to get hold of the Minister. I'll have to take this." He put his hand on the cassette player.

The lawyer's slight frame seemed to be recharged with energy. "Hang on! In the meantime I've got an innocent client sitting in a cell in Holloway."

Suthern moved his head from side to side. "There's nothing we can do tonight. In any case, with luck she'll be sleeping. We'll have her out first thing in the morning."

He picked up the phone, dialed, and spoke briefly. "The

Minister's still in the House. I'll go straight there. I'm going to enjoy this, Patrick. I spoke to some pompous clown at the Yard after I left you. They wouldn't hear a word against Hackett."

They all stood as he rose, Raven with a sense of déjà vu. It was like being in church, the statue, the priest, and the small group of believers.

Suthern's lack of height forced him to look up at Raven. "You'd better lie low until morning. It'll take a few hours to get things straightened out officially."

"He can stay here," O'Callaghan said quickly. The lawyer's apartment was up on the next floor.

"And the lady," said Suthern, turning to Mrs. Drake. "I'd like her moved somewhere safe until Hackett's behind bars."

O'Callaghan went down the stairs with him. The sound of a car being driven away drifted through the open door. Then the lawyer was back.

"We'll put you in a hotel," he said to Mildred Drake.

By now she was totally immersed in her role in the drama. Bracelets rattled around her wrist as she touched Keglevic's sleeve.

"Will you drive me home to collect my things?"

Keglevic glanced over at Raven. "Jacek will drive you home," said Raven. He paused for a minute. "And he'll take you to your hotel."

Patrick O'Callaghan put down the phone. "The room's booked. It's the Cumberland."

17

IT WAS FIVE O'CLOCK and already dark when Hackett drove the Datsun out to Forest Hill. He used a pay phone outside the station but there was no reply to the number he dialed. He climbed back behind the wheel, lit a cheroot, and moved the pickup to the top of the Crescent. He sat there for a while, looking across at Mildred Drake's house. There were no lights showing. He slipped across the street and down the flagged pathway. The end of a newspaper was sticking out from the letterbox.

He walked around behind the house and peered through the dirty kitchen window. A tap dripped below. There was enough light to see a dirty glass and coffee cup in the sink. He stepped back, looking up at the second story. The place projected the empty silence of a house that was unoccupied. He made his way back to the pickup. Wherever she was, she hadn't been bluffing.

If you really want to see me, come to the party tomorrow night. It's on John Raven's houseboat, seven o'clock.

He imagined the sneer on her face as she said it. No, Mildred never bluffed. She planted the shiv surely and then twisted it. He stared across at the house with hatred. His brain seemed to be only partly lit. Some of the circuits had tripped. Those that still worked were focused on Mildred's destruction. Again and again came the thought — she could have let him off the hook but chose to betray him instead.

The deer rifle was under the front seat, the handgun stuffed in his overcoat pocket. He'd probably get only one shot at her but that was all that really mattered. If he managed to get anyone else, Raven, whoever, it would be a bonus. He started back north, his mind no longer thinking logically but that made sense. Where he was now, there was no room for logic. Logic meant walking into the nearest police station and giving himself up. Logic meant standing in the dock charged with murder. Logic was serving life imprisonment, rubbing shoulders with villains he had sent to jail. His way out was already determined, resting in the right-hand pocket of his overcoat with a shell in the breech.

He was over Battersea Bridge now with the arc of street lamps curving along the embankment toward Raven's house-boat. He was about to swing right when he saw the parked car at the bottom of Beaufort Street facing the flotilla of boats. He trod hard on the gas, recognizing the one-way rear windows of a Flying Squad vehicle. There was an F.M. band on the Datsun radio. He switched on and fiddled the dial, trying for a police broadcast. He found it as he neared Fulham Road, hearing his own name mentioned twice with a code number. Three Six Two. *To be approached with extreme caution.*

He turned right, ran a couple of blocks before heading back toward the river. There had to be a stakeout on Raven's boat. His own vehicles had been called off two days ago. He parked as close as he could to the river, on a side street running into the embankment. There were no police cars in sight. Danger would come when he ran the gauntlet to the parking lot next to the pub. He locked the pickup and walked, his coat collar turned up again, the felt hat pulled low. The lights were bright along the embankment. It was a no-parking area for a quarter mile in both directions. There was no place for a car loaded with armed police-marksmen to remain inconspicuous. *To be approached with extreme caution.* They'd be wearing bulletproof vests. The bridges and the pub parking lot would be the obvious places for the stakeout. Hackett turned left and cut through side streets to the bottom of Oakley

Street. The second police car was parked in the angle of Cheyne Walk, lights out and with no one but the driver evident.

Hackett turned on his heel and continued walking back along the embankment, steeling himself as he neared the glow of the pub windows. High tide had lifted the small group of boats. Hackett could see them without turning his head. Whatever other precautions had been taken, Raven had no worries about showing himself. Every light was burning on the *Albatross* and the curtains had been left undrawn. Hackett was abreast of the pub by now. Trees grew along the back of the parking lot. A dim sign located an outside lavatory. Hackett walked into the urinal and out again. There were only two cars on the dark stretch of hardtop. One was a sleek Corniche, the other a family Morris. He moved a few yards closer to the river. He had a good view of the *Albatross* from where he stood. The long sitting room was crowded with people drinking champagne. He could see the bottles on the table, Raven and Kirstie Macfarlane moving around, Jerry Soo, the lawyer. Mildred Drake was framed in a window, chatting to a tall stranger with the build of a bear. Mildred's hair had been done and she was clearly making an effort.

Hackett's mouth thinned. He wouldn't find a better place than where he was standing. He took the short cut through the bars and out onto the embankment. He unlocked the pickup and removed the deer rifle from its case. His overcoat concealed it as he walked back to the parking lot. The Morris was still there but the Corniche had been replaced by a repair truck. Hackett walked straight through the pub and into the shadows. Nothing could stop him now. He took off his gloves and rested the rifle on top of the Morris. Mildred Drake was still framed in the window. Suddenly the lights faded, like the close of a scene on the stage. From bright to dim, leaving only the glow of candlelight.

Death walked in Hackett's head and he sighted carefully,

finger crooking on the trigger. *Now!* said the voice. His finger squeezed gently but firmly. The butt recoiled against his shoulder, the sound of the explosion splitting the traffic and rebounding from the river. There was an eerie hush as if people were waiting for the end of the world. Then the parking lot flared with light. Hackett threw the rifle into the trees. His pistol was halfway to his mouth when the repair truck roared across, headlights blazing. The front end knocked Hackett off balance. A heavy weight hit him in the back of the head. The last thing he heard before losing consciousness was the banshee wail of a police siren.

18

RAVEN had filled the long room with flowers, roses to welcome Kirstie home. Their color and scent filled the houseboat. The Krug had been on ice since late afternoon. Mrs. Burrows was handing around canapés with an air of relief mixed with her customary disapproval. Only one person had canceled the invitation. Neil Suthern had to attend a meeting. All the others were there. Patrick O'Callaghan, dapper in an Edwardian-styled suit with cuffs and wearing a patterned-silk waistcoat. Jerry Soo was in his Detective-Inspector's outfit. His smile looked as if it had been baked onto his face permanently. Keglevic and Mildred Drake were very much a couple, chatting away by the window. If Hanka ever got wind of it, thought Raven, she'd retrieve her little pistol and deal with the situation.

Raven refilled his glass. The ice-cold bubbles exploded against his palate and gums. Kirstie was still wearing her cords and baggy-necked sweater. O'Callaghan had slept little last night, putting Raven to bed on the divan in the spare room and working the phone nonstop for the next two hours. They had gone to the Yard together at ten o'clock in the morning. Raven's statement proved to run over 6,000 words, each one of them watched by O'Callaghan with the dedicated care of a surgeon. It was after eleven when they left the building with Raven officially a free man. Their first task was to retrieve Raven's car from the Police Pound. The machinery to unlock Kirstie's cell proved to be more complicated than they had expected. They spent the afternoon driving from the Home Office to the Prison Commissioner's and back, getting signatures and disclaimers until at five o'clock the release was ready. They delivered it to Holloway. The prison governor had already been notified and Kirstie was waiting. She sat beside Raven on the way back to the houseboat, silent after the first flurry of words. O'Callaghan was in the back seat. From time to time, Raven glanced up at the rearview mirror. When his eyes met Kirstie's, she turned her head. She seemed on the verge of speaking but no words came. It was clear that something was troubling her.

*

He glanced across the room at her now, talking to Patrick and Soo. She'd had no time to change or do much to her face. Her hair was tied in a loose knot that lolled on the back of her neck. He crossed and took her arm.

"Do you mind if I borrow her?" he asked.

O'Callaghan turned to Soo. "Shall we let him?"

Soo spoke through his smile. "He's an ugly man if he's crossed. I hear rumors of violence."

Raven closed the bedroom door on them. Her unpacked bag was on the floor.

"Sit down, darling." His voice was tender.

She sat on the edge of the bed. He looked at her, trying to read her eyes.

"You blame me for everything, don't you?" he challenged. "That's what's bugging you, isn't it?"

There were purple smudges beneath her eyes and she looked very tired. "I blame nobody," she said. "It's just that three days in prison made me realize that I'm not really cut out for this kind of life." She turned her hand over slowly as if to offer further explanation.

They sat there looking at one another, the boat rocking gently, bearing the familiar sounds that were part of their life together.

"Those things you wanted?" he said suddenly. "Do they still matter?"

She raised her head again. "Not unless they matter to you."

"They matter," he said.

A small smile surrounded her lips. "You mean you're prepared to pay the price?"

"I'm buying a boat," he said. "Will you marry me?"

"What kind of a boat?" Her eyes had changed, grown darker.

He took the clipping from his pocket. "A thirteen-meter wooden ketch with a Volvo fifty-horsepower engine. She sleeps two. You can name her."

"You just convinced me," she said. "Yes, I'll marry you."

Her lips were cool but firm against his. He led her back into the sitting room and cut the lights, leaving only the candles burning in the branched silver holders. Then he clapped his hands for attention.

"Will you please fill your glasses? We have an announcement to make. Kirstie's just agreed to make an honest man of me."

"And about time too!" Patrick O'Callaghan was first off the mark. Others crowded around, raising glasses, offering congratulations. Mrs. Burrows was tearfully slopping champagne. A sliver of moon showed through the undrawn curtains. Keglevic and Mildred were still by the window engrossed in one another. Raven released Kirstie's hand.

"Mildred hasn't had a drink all evening."

Kirstie grinned. She had shed ten years in the last five minutes.

"She's trying to do the right thing."

"The hell with that," said Raven and turned. "Mildred!" he called.

She lifted her hand and waved. "Didn't you hear what I said?" he asked. "Or are you too busy listening to that ugly Pole? Kirstie and I are going to be married. You simply have to drink a glass of champagne!"

She glanced up at Keglevic, as shy as a girl. Raven took a full glass from Mrs. Burrows' tray.

"Give it to her, darling," he said to Kirstie.

Kirstie took the glass, walking with the movement of the boat so as not to spill the drink. The two women moved toward one another, laughing as the glass went from hand to hand.

The window exploded. The shell took Mildred in the side of the neck. She pitched forward as Raven ran to catch her. Bright arterial blood pumped over his hands and clothing, discoloring her face. Raven lifted her onto the sofa.

19

THEY WERE IN ONE of the upstairs bars. The rain outside laid a sheet of black glass across the tarmac. It was barely four o'clock in the afternoon but the navigational lights were burning brightly on the runways.

Jerry Soo had driven Kirstie and Raven to Heathrow and the three of them sat now with their drinks untouched. They had been silent for the last twenty minutes. It was Raven who finally broke the silence, staring out at the gathering darkness.

"Well, I suppose it's as good a day as any to leave all this behind. Assuming that you have to do it."

"I have to do it," said Kirstie.

Soo's face was that of an ivory figure on a mantelpiece. "Toronto," he said glumly. "Earmuffs and electrical shocks every time you get out of the bathtub. And all that bloody snow."

Kirstie's chin lifted, her eyes understanding. "It's not as bad as you make it sound. In any case I want to go home."

"She wants to go home," said Raven. "It's as simple as that. In any case we'll be back for the trial. That's only five weeks."

"Why is it," Soo demanded, "that I always have to do your dirty work? Now I have to break the news to Louise that you people are getting married three thousand miles away! She's going to want to know why I let you do it. Come to think of it, why *am* I letting you do it?"

Raven moved his head uncertainly. "Louise won't make problems. All you have to do is keep an eye on Mrs. Burrows and the boat."

Soo removed his hand from his anorak pocket. When he opened his fingers, there was a wedding ring fashioned from three slim gold bands in his palm. He slid the ring across the tabletop to Kirstie.

"See that he uses it. The wedding won't be legal unless."

She slipped it onto her finger then removed it hurriedly. "I love you, Jerry Soo," she said quietly.

"Me too," he said. "And don't let him bully you."

A metallic voice sounded in the Tannoy. "This is the final call for passengers taking Air Canada Flight Seven Four Three to Toronto. Will passengers who have not yet boarded the aircraft please go to Gate Eleven immediately!"

Raven picked up his shoulder bag. "That's us, Kirstie. Let's go."

Even in flat heels, Kirstie was taller than the Chinese cop. She kissed him once on the forehead.

"Take care of yourself, Jerry."

The two men shook hands as they always did, briefly but firmly. "That's right," said Raven. "You take care of yourself."

"I don't even have an address," Soo complained.

"Nor do we," said Raven. "Don't worry. We'll be all right."

Soo's square grin broke and held. "You probably will, dammit. With your kind of luck you probably will. In any case, you've got as much chance as anyone else."

Raven watched him through the doorway. Kirstie's voice was quiet beside him. "But I love you most of all, John Raven."

He looked at her for fully thirty seconds before he smiled. "That's going to help," he said. "That's going to help a lot!"